CARETAKER

The Goodpasture Chronicles

R.J. Halbert

Eald Talu House

To Kelton & Kennedy, may the stories of our past guide you to a life of joy and freedom in your future.

Caretaker
The Goodpasture Chronicles

Copyright © 2023 by R.J. Halbert

ISBN (Paperback Edition): 978-1-963366-04-4

Published by:
Eald Talu House
(A Division of Novus Press Works)
Nashville, TN 37212

To Jason, my best friend, my life-long love, and the best and most colorful part of my story. Oh, the many adventures you have taken me on! I dedicate this book to my mother Nancy, who always had a flair for drama, humor, and spiritual matters. She used what little energy she had left to speak a blessing over me as her life was ending in a tragic way. Her selfless last act led to a new awakening in my spirit. For that, I am forever grateful.

I love you and miss you, Mom.

- Rhonda Halbert

I descend from a long line of storytellers. As a child, I was always surrounded by fabulous tales, impossible dreams, and fantastical journeys. Tales of wolves in the night, leprechauns driving tiny cars through the streets, secret missions across Checkpoint Charlie, and a tank-driving Nana. It never occurred to me that some of them might not be true, until I was much older. I remember the first time recounting tales of my family's experiences growing up in post-World War II Europe, and seeing the look of slight disbelief in my friend's eyes. As it turns out, they were all true—mostly. My family had a way of turning intense trauma into adventure. God consistently turned the most dire circumstances around in moments my mom called "but suddenly." I've continued that adventure with the love of my life, Rhonda, and we've brought our children up in the same sense of wonder my mom instilled in me. After our world was turned upside down one traumatic event after another, the only way we knew to process it was to tell our stories. Though this one is not entirely true, the lessons we learned and our faith in the coming "but suddenly" are firmly rooted in reality. I miss you and love you so much, Mom. Thank you for teaching us how to tell (and live) a tale.

Ultimately, our stories are our testimony.

- Jason Halbert

CONTENTS

Prologue

*T*HE SUN REFLECTS *off the river, glistening onto the armor of soldiers patrolling the great city walls. Sandstone houses line the stone-paved street, so close to one another that some share a wall with their neighbor. A young boy darts through the narrow spaces between the homes, saying "hello" as he passes familiar faces inside or waving to the townspeople standing on streets lined with vendors selling wine, baskets, baked goods, and oils. He spends most of his days playing along the Jordan River, exploring the fjords leading to lush, fertile crops and small forests. When he isn't exploring, he is reading or helping his parents.*

He is an energetic and curious young boy, thin and tall with a head full of curly dark hair. He is also the youngest in his family, the only boy. His two older sisters spend most of their days pursuing their education or working with their mother, assisting as she tends to the high priestess and eldest daughter of the King. His father, a trusted advisor to the King, was a childhood friend of the royal before his ascent to power. Because of their long-standing relationship, the boy's parents are tasked with tending to the temple that houses their most powerful ancient deity. Even at this early age he is aware it is he who will be expected to carry on this honored position after his parents are no longer able.

The main roadway, Procession Street, leads to the northern gate of the temple. There are several other gates around the enormous structure, which is protected by an outer wall. Standing at the entrance and looking up at the massive winding staircase leading to the different layers within would be daunting to most young children. But the young boy is not intimidated. To him, it is all too familiar. When his mother accompanies the High Priestess, they often enter through the royal gate on the east side. The tall tower is known to those who live within the walls of the city as the passageway to heaven. It is a place to honor and bask in the presence of their God.

He spends hours inside the temple while his parents fulfill their duties, offering water, food, and incense as an act of devotion. While most of his friends spend their days playing by the river, he prefers learning and perfecting the intricate rituals. For as long as he can remember, he has listened to his mother and the High Priestess talk about this God; His strengths and ability to harness the power of the past.

This day begins like most. He approaches his mother and hands her the unblemished fruit he carefully selected from the street vendor just moments before. She puts the fruit into her basket as she packs the necessary items for today's ritual. His two sisters are also preparing baskets. All three are going to the temple with the High Priestess. His mother insists he join them.

After helping his mother with the offering, he asks if he can take a break. She knows he likes to explore while she works, so she gives him permission to do so with an admonition to not venture too far. After playing for an hour, tucked behind a wall, he hears a rush of footsteps and passing voices. He peeks his head around the corner of the entrance to the temple and sees his father frantically searching for his mother.

He follows close enough not to lose his father, but far enough to not be caught. He watches as his father stops and speaks with other advisors, who are also frantically searching for their families. Seeing the panic in his father's face, the boy reveals himself.

"Papa, they are inside the temple placing the offerings."

His father grabs him and rushes to find the rest of the family, carrying the young boy under his arm. Each time they come across others, his father tells them to flee the city, beyond the walls. He is decisive but calm.

Something is terribly wrong.

ONE

"**B**EDU OR BEDOUIN, as you may know them, remain one of the world's most ancient, yet misunderstood, cultures. These nomadic tribes have survived the harsh conditions of the desert for centuries, yet their origins have been difficult to trace as they have left little evidence behind for archeologists."

Ian paused to allow the translator to catch up and to let his head further settle from the residual effects of a hangover. Fighting the fog that threatened to steal his focus, he scanned the audience, attempting to gauge their interest in his lecture contrasting their worldview with that of a culture often perceived by modern society as a lesser people.

"Mainly found in the Arabian and Syrian deserts, the Sinai in Egypt, and the Sahara, the Bedouin developed a rich tapestry of religious beliefs and perspectives that some believe set the foundation for many of today's religions around the world. To make sense of our current understanding of Goodness, let's take a step back in time and observe our world through the lens of the Bedu. Unlike our modern contemporaries, the Bedouin were not given to convenience nor luxury—and I believe this was not due to lack of opportunity."

1

As the translator again interpreted his remarks to the attendees, one hand hovered above the mouse, ready to click to the next slide while he nearly pinched himself with the other. Even a throbbing headache couldn't diminish the awe he felt that he was actually there.

For Ian Keane, Professor of Ancient History at Boston University, it had always been a lifelong dream to speak at the historic Seeon Abbey in Bavaria, Germany. And now there he was, standing in front of a packed house, in a building built in 994 A.D., discussing an ancient people he had spent years researching and studying. He glanced again at the listeners, a mixture of students and fellow researchers. It was a diverse group, and everyone seemed to be focused intently on the translation of his words. As he scanned the crowd, he felt a presence from just off the wings of the stage, thinking he caught a familiar face in the corner of his eye. But when he turned his full attention to the side, there was no one there.

He shook off the distraction as just one more lingering effect of drinking too much the night before, took a deep breath and continued.

"One early Arabic scholar believed that sedentary life constituted the last stage of civilization, the point where it began to decay. It was in this spirit that the Bedouin fought to avoid the yoke of 'the city'. If you'll indulge me a moment, let's narrow in on the Qashqa'i tribe, as I have come to believe it was this specific tribe that ..."

He stopped suddenly, distracted by a message alert from his laptop. He paused, cueing the translator to

take over, then clicked on the alert to make sure everything was okay.

It's time. I found it!

TWO

ONE HUNDRED AND forty-four miles, three hours, sixteen minutes, two bathroom stops. The kids had already asked, "Are we there yet?" at least a half dozen times, but for Lyana Keane, the hours had slipped along almost unnoticed as swirls of anticipation intensified with each passing mile marker. Her dreams were coming to life in front of her eyes on the open road between Boston and Littleton, New Hampshire, interrupted only by the occasional glance in the passenger side mirror.

Objects in mirror are closer than they appear.

Lyana looked over at her husband, Ian, and offered a smile that was equal parts appreciation and apprehension, but he was so focused on the road ahead he didn't notice. Her eyes fell on the words in the mirror again.

A tear welled up in the corner of her eye as she thought about what they would leave behind with this move—the history, the adventure.

The loss.

A hazy picture of downtown Boston forms in the mirror. The high-rises are melting like hot wax, disappearing one by one. *We lost sight of the city hours ago* ... Lyana puzzles over the strange transformation—

Stop. Not now.

Jolted back to reality as Ian hit a pothole, Lyana's left hand reflexively grabbed the seat to steady herself, as the other clutched her necklace, stopping it from swinging.

"Are you with me?" Ian asked, removing his right hand from the steering wheel to gently grasp her arm. She nearly jumped again at his touch.

"Oh! Uh ... yeah. I'm fine. I just thought I saw something." Lyana forced a smile then turned to hide her face. The pain still lingered.

Will this ever get easier?

Lyana turned to look at the kids sitting in the back seat, Ariel, who shared her father's fair skin and light-colored hair, a gift of his Irish roots, and Zach, clearly his mother's son with curly brown hair and hints of her Persian heritage, but with his father's freckles and green eyes—then dropped her shoulders and sighed. *They will be fine,* she thought. *They'll see—this house is exactly what we all need. I'm sure of it.*

The GPS read seven miles to their destination. Six miles ... five miles ... four miles.

Lyana listened as Zach, still over-stimulated from recently celebrating his twelfth birthday, echoed the numbers being called out by the GPS. Ariel, their fifteen-year-old daughter, looked up from her journal she'd been writing in to see Zach grinning from ear to ear as he surveyed the changing scenery. It appeared to Lyana that for once, Ariel wasn't annoyed by her brother's constant interruptions. She could sense Ariel was feeling the same butterflies flitting around her stomach as she was. The feeling that washed over her—and perhaps all of them—was one she hadn't felt in quite some time.

The thrill of the unknown.

Nestled on the edge of the White Mountains, the quaint town on the Connecticut river unfolded before them as they turned off the freeway. The view reminded Lyana of a Norman Rockwell painting, complete with American flags, colorful, time-etched buildings, and streets alive with activity. Neighbors greeted each other as they meandered along the sidewalks, popping in and out of shops. They slowed as they neared a covered bridge and Lyana watched children playing kickball in a nearby park. She rolled down her window and listened to the melody of children's laughter accompanied by the babbling river. Beyond the bridge, they came upon an old mill, the river and time chipping away at its beautiful red façade. It was more than just a quaint town to Lyana, it was idyllic. She took in the sights and scents of the small town and knew this was the right place for her family.

Lyana had been increasingly eager to leave the hustle of the city and find a place where their family could slow down and reconnect with one another. So, when she found the house during a random internet search a few days prior, she decided they would make the trip as soon as Ian returned from the conference in Germany, not even waiting to discuss it with him before making an appointment with the realtor.

She had almost skipped over the listing the first time she saw it, thinking it would be too far out of their price range given the size of the property and number of rooms. But as she caught her reflection in the monitor, she thought she heard a whisper.

You need this.

She paused, convinced she'd imagined the voice, then continued to study the listing. With each click, her excitement grew. When she walked through the house on a virtual tour, she knew this was the one.

And now, they were moments away from seeing it in person for the first time.

Lyana had been nervous to show the listing to Ian, but her worries were dismissed when he smiled at the first image on the screen—an aerial shot of Littleton. "It's like a scene right out of the books I've been teaching from," he told her, before reaching across and clicking the "next" button. Though his initial thesis during grad school focused on the tent-dwelling Bedouin culture, his studies led him to become somewhat of an expert on how tribal communities influenced the creation of towns and villages in ancient times. After years of listening as her husband passionately recounted his experiences traveling Europe and the Middle East, Lyana was convinced the small town flanked by lush and rolling hills to the left, the river to the right and the historically preserved downtown lined with local shops and eateries would tug on all his senses. As she watched him click to the last picture on the listing, she wasn't entirely surprised when he finally said, "I can see why you love it so much. It's kind of amazing."

Lyana felt something she hadn't in a long time when he spoke those words: hope.

As they slowly drove through Main Street, taking it all in, that hope was blossoming into something palpable. She peered out the window at all the charming businesses—the barber shop, the soda shop, boutiques, cafés, an antiques store. Not much different from her own hometown. A bright glint of sunlight on glass grabbed her attention. Following the light, she caught her own reflection in one of the store-front windows.

Marching in the Heritage Festival Parade had always been a dream for Lyana. As a young child she would stand on the side of the street watching the band and majorettes march by in perfect unison to the rhythm of the drums, and she desperately wanted to be a part of that. Now is her chance. With growing excitement, she lifts the flute and plays her part with confidence and pride. As she approaches the intersection where she knows her family would be, she sees her mom videotaping her and her sister jumping up and down and waving. Her stepfather hadn't even bothered to stand up. He is lounging in a rusty lawn chair on the sidewalk with his beer in his hand, reading the newspaper.

Stop it, Lyana ... Today is not the day.

Lyana shook the intrusive thoughts away and refocused on her surroundings. The further they travelled away from downtown, the more serene the surroundings felt. The streets were lined with historic homes, perfectly manicured lawns, and lush, tree-filled rolling foothills in the background.

Three miles … two miles … one mile.

Right on cue, Boston's "More than a Feeling" came on the radio. Lyana looked back just in time to see Ariel and Zach sharing a sibling moment, rolling their eyes as she and Ian mimed the iconic opening guitar riff. They sang along in full voice.

I looked out this morning and the sun was gone
Turned on some music to start the day
I lost myself in a familiar song
I closed my eyes and I slipped away

The music continued as they made their way towards the house.

It's more than a feeling {More than a feeling}
When I hear that old song they used to play {More than a feeling}
I begin dreaming {More than a feeling}

"Re-routing," the voice from the GPS chimed in.

They had missed the turn while basking in their musical glory days. Ian turned around and headed back the way they'd come. Within minutes, the GPS left them baffled once again.

"Re-routing. Please make a U-turn ahead."

"I don't understand. It says it should be right here, Lyana," said Ian.

"You must not have been paying attention. Turn around and I'll look to the right. You look left."

"Re-routing. Please make a U-turn ahead."

"Argh! This is the same stretch we just did. See there's nothi—"

They turned around one more time, before finally spotting the nearly hidden driveway that was numerically out of order and barely marked.

They turned down the driveway and entered what looked like a gateway into another world. Bushes were thick on each side, leaving just enough room for the car to pass. Only a few brave rays of sunlight broke through the shadowy trees that lined the narrow path. Ian drove for what seemed like miles.

"Where is the house?" asked Zach. His voice was almost a whisper.

The sky grew dark and low-hanging fog marched toward them, making it difficult to see in the distance. It was mid-morning, but it might as well have been dusk. An uneasy hush settled throughout the car. The change in scenery from the quaint downtown they had just experienced was stark; this was the opposite of what she had hoped to find. Lyana needed this to be so much more than a new beginning, or a fresh start.

Trying to make sense of it all, tears began to gather in Lyana's eyes. The sudden shift in the car from hopeful expectation to uncertainty triggered painful memories of the devastation and heartbreak she felt after the loss of her mother earlier that year. On top of living through *the unthinkable* only a few years earlier, the heartbreak of losing her mother nearly pushed her over the edge. Even though their relationship was strained, in her culture family was everything. Each generation was deeply connected to the next and losing her mom felt like a vast piece of her was gone forever.

Lyana had been an outsider in her small Irish community with her long dark hair, olive complexion, and brown eyes. Her family moved to the area in pursuit of the American Dream and had lived there for years, several generations calling it home. She was the first one to leave.

From the very beginning she and Ian knew it wouldn't be an easy road for two small-town kids looking to pave their own way and leave life in that small town behind, breaking free from the generational expectations attached to them within the confines of a twenty-mile radius. They were so young and naïve—they believed just walking away from where it all began would give them a chance to fix the brokenness within. That belief crumbled in the months leading up to the night Lyana had taken the kids and left. Ian had come too close to repeating the mistakes of his father. It was the darkest season of life they had known. Once again, she was the first one to leave.

This is a different kind of leaving, she thought.

Lyana glanced at Ian again, hoping he hadn't noticed her tears. Thankfully, he appeared as transfixed as she with the curious surroundings.

How long is this guitar solo? Feels like it's been on for hours!

Lyana felt Ian's touch again and she looked over to him and smiled as their fingertips met.

"Lyana, I know it's ..." Before Ian could finish his thought, the radio suddenly scrambled into static.

Zach screamed.

"What was that?" Ariel asked.

Lyana turned to see Zach covering his ears. It was his way of dealing with unexpected noises. She assured him that everything was fine, then quickly returned her attention to the front windshield as Ian slowed the car to a stop. Ahead of them was a vast, black iron fence. The gates were flung open, and weeds had taken hold of them, assuring they'd stay that way, but an arch loomed above the driveway. It had been overrun with thick vines and was marked in the center with the rusting remnants of a crest. The years had taken a toll on the paint, making the emblem hard to make out, but as they passed under the arch, Zach read the inscription aloud.

"Meritus Augentur Honores."

Cautiously, they continued forward. As they cleared the gate, the trees finally stepped aside, revealing a grassy clearing. At first, all Lyana could see was the fog, but then a lamp-post appeared out of the mist.

"Are we in Narnia?" asked Ariel. There was the hint of a smile in her words.

"I think maybe we are," said Ian, sounding genuinely surprised. He pulled further up the driveway and the house made its first appearance—a ghost coming to life before them. It was somehow both grand and intimate at the same time. It oozed with history and mystery.

And possibility.

It's perfect.

The thought came to her like a whisper.

THREE

J UNE SIGNALED THE beginning of the busy summer tourist season, full of festivals and weekend travelers looking for a quaint getaway. For realtor Kelly Garner, it meant increased traffic and hopefully an upswing in business following the market crash just six months before.

As she opened the glass door to the vestibule of the Littleton Café, a favorite coffee spot and diner for locals, her face was buried in her phone. She sent off a text and entered through the second door. When she looked up from her phone, she nodded at her colleague and friend, Angela Daughtry, who was already sipping her coffee at their usual table.

Kelly and Angela had reconnected after Kelly returned home to Littleton following a divorce and major life transition. Angela was the Managing Broker for Hope at Home Realty and graciously took Kelly under her wing. The two had worked together ever since.

"Latte, please," said Kelly, but she really didn't need to say anything at all. The Littleton Café had been owned by the Warner family for years and was the type of place where everyone knew your name *and* your order.

"Already on it!" Lloyd smiled and pointed to the espresso machine.

Moments later, Kelly grabbed her coffee and headed over to Angela. She sat down across from her and let out a sigh. "Another day, another showing."

"Farr Hill?"

"You guessed it! I have a good feeling about it."

"That's what you said last time."

Kelly sighed again and smiled. "I know."

The house on the hill was a rarity for local realtors: a house that wouldn't sell. In one of the busiest housing markets they had ever experienced, they just couldn't find a buyer for the Tudor house tucked away in the woods.

Originally built in 1933, the manor on Farr Hill was a unique blend of masonry and woodwork, combined with a beautiful asymmetrical roof, which made it an uncommon find amongst the uniform architecture of the picturesque town. In the mid-nineteenth century, as stereoscopes experienced a boom in popularity, Littleton emerged as the central manufacturing town of this new entertainment and educational device. By 1860, the local factory was at its peak, churning out over 3,000 stereoscopic views a day. The influx of workers and their families resulted in a surge of new homes being built in the common Victorian style of the time, making the old English manor later built by Mr. Goodpasture an architectural anomaly.

Not much was known of Mr. Goodpasture's life before moving to Littleton. He was an antiques dealer and incredibly skilled craftsman, but for the most part he kept to himself. When he mysteriously disappeared in 1973, Mr.

Goodpasture's nephew, Marshall, took over the property and became the official groundskeeper. The locals began inventing tall tales about the house as they watched family upon family move in and out, none staying long enough to become fully invested in the community. The stories ranged from the somewhat believable ("it has unreliable plumbing") to the familiar East Coast mythos ("it's haunted"). It had now sat empty for nearly two years since the last owners moved.

"I have a family coming in from Boston today. Fingers crossed!"

Angela responded with a smirk. "Good luck with that."

Looking down at her phone again, Kelly gathered her purse and coffee. She started typing a message. "Looks like they're already there. I guess they made better time than they'd expected. Someone else is showing the house this morning, too, so I texted them to hang on until it's our turn to view the house."

"You better hustle, then," said Angela. She lifted her coffee cup. "Let me know how the showing goes."

Kelly took a long sip of her latte and exited the diner, feeling that all-too-familiar twist of hope and anxiety.

FOUR

LYANA STOOD THERE stunned. Pictures hadn't done the house justice. As the sun burned off the fog and the house materialized out of the mist, the only word that came to mind was magnificent. It was grand—from the Tudor architecture to the lush gardens surrounding stone fountains and the vast forest behind it. It was like they had been transported to another world, another era.

Every detail was perfect. The immense, well-worn beams framing the stonework on the first floor and the stucco on the upper level, vintage stained-glass windows, ancient-looking front door, antique black-iron sconce, and the tendrils of brown and green ivy weaving their tale across the stone chimney. There was so much history to behold. The elegant, ten-foot tall lamp-post loomed like a lighthouse, calling Lyana safely home.

She could not wait to go inside. A car pulled up behind theirs and a woman got out.

"Hello, you must be the Keane family," the woman said as she extended her hand to Lyana and then Ian. She offered a smile to Ariel and Zach. "I'm Kelly. So sorry I didn't get here before you."

"No apology necessary," said Ian. "We just made better time than I'd expected."

Kelly smiled and nodded toward the house. "You probably noticed the other cars—we're a few minutes early and there is another family touring the house, so maybe we can walk the grounds ..."

But before she finished her sentence, the front door opened and a couple made a quick exit, followed by someone who looked every bit the prototypical real estate agent—pleated skirt, matching neutral-toned blazer over a white blouse and expensive-looking, but sensible shoes. Lyana guessed the BMW in the driveway was hers. She caught some of the conversation between the potential buyers as they walked to their SUV.

"The ceiling felt so low, and it didn't have much natural light," said the woman. The man—*her husband?* wondered Lyana—just nodded, a scowl revealing not only his reply but his overall assessment of the property.

Lyana's gut twisted again. She felt like she was on a rollercoaster ride—from hope to disappointment and back to hope again—and now dipping back into disappointment. It was hard to keep up. She noticed the two realtors exchange a look, then Kelly turned to Lyana and Ian.

"Ready to go in?" She wore the kind of smile Lyana recognized as something that took effort. She'd worn more than a few of those smiles over the years.

They walked to the front door, their heels clicking against a brick footpath that looked as though it had seen decades of use. Lyana marveled at the intricate carving on the front door—not a fleur-de-lis, but something else—something curious and clearly old. She glanced at the array of small windows in the door that promised a tease of what was inside, but only saw her reflection staring back.

Welcome …

The squeak of old hinges startled Lyana.

"Welcome to Farr Hill," said Kelly, gesturing for them to enter.

Lyana didn't know what to expect. The previous couple sure didn't like what they'd seen.

Kelly immediately started pointing out features of the house, paying special attention to all the modernization that had been done to the house. "Appliances are mostly all new," she said, walking briskly ahead as if on a tight schedule. But Lyana wasn't interested in racing through the house—she was compelled to linger in her first impression. Her fears lifted immediately. The house didn't feel cramped or claustrophobic—it felt warm, inviting. She lagged behind the rest of them as Kelly did her best to sell them on the house's unique charm. Lyana didn't need Kelly's words to convince her. As she ran her fingers gently across the textured wall, a smile came to her face. She took in the exposed beams and brick, then turned to catch the sun glowing through the windows, their wooden grilles painting checkerboards along the floor.

"It has so much … character," said Lyana. Kelly paused her spiel and turned to Lyana, a curious expression on her face. Just as quickly, her lips formed into a smile. Not the realtor kind of smile, but a real one.

Lyana followed the group into the kitchen and noted the aforementioned "updated appliances", but was struck mostly by the marble counters—not the bar height ones found in most newer homes, but shorter, the height of a traditional dinner table. She closed her eyes and brushed her fingers across the cool surface, imagining the family dinners they would share together there.

Everything cried out to be touched.

There was a surprising warmth and familiarity about this place, she thought. Lyana felt an inexplicable connection to the property.

"Lyana, you need to see this."

Still floating in her daydream, Lyana followed Ian's voice to find him in the back room off the second open living space. A door that looked like it was from the eighteenth century opened to a stone-walled room that faced east with a clear view of the small creek that ran off the river. Beams of dark wood embedded in the stone ran from the floor to the ceiling both vertically and at a slight angle, making the room look almost medieval.

"I mean, this is perfect for my office," he said, beaming.

"And for your morning coffee," added Lyana. She could almost taste the coffee herself as she breathed in the scent of stone and old wood. Her breath caught when she noticed the large painting that hung on one of the walls. It appeared to be a rendition of the very room they stood in, or at least nearly so. Because it was painted with the same browns and grays of the room, she had nearly missed it.

"Does the painting come with the house?" she asked Kelly, who was practically beaming by now.

"Oh, I'm sure something can be arranged," she said.

"We're going upstairs to check out the bedrooms," said Ariel. She and Zach raced to the stairs. Lyana stared at the painting for another beat, then followed Ian out of the room and over to the grand staircase.

Zach took his time, counting each stair on the way up.

"… 13, 14, 15!" he exclaimed when he reached the landing.

It wasn't quite a two-story house, noted Lyana as she approached the upstairs hallway. The ceilings were sloped and angled with varying heights following the roof line. It made for cozy nook areas throughout.

"This one's mine," said Ariel, peeking out of a bedroom doorway. Zach walked out of the room he had claimed and joined Ariel in hers. Lyana stepped in to see the space Ariel had chosen as her own.

"Oh, cool," said Ariel. She had just spied the Sixties era intercom that Lyana had noticed were scattered all around the house. "I wonder if it works …" Ariel punched a button on the device and loud screech followed by static rang through the house. Zach jumped and covered his ears, then began pacing back and forth. When he'd sufficiently calmed himself, he spoke firmly to Ariel.

"You can't just turn it up like that. You need to adjust it first. Like this." He turned and went back into his chosen room.

"Check one. Check two. Can you hear me? Over." Zach's muffled voice filtered into the room on the intercom speaker.

"Whoa! I can hear you," Ariel yelled out the door.

Zach's voice came across the intercom again. "No, you have to press the button to talk to me, Ariel! Press the button labeled *Green Room*. I think that's mine."

Ariel pressed the Green Room button. "Ah! I hear you loud and clear little buddy. This is so cool! Over," Ariel called back.

Their intercom game continued for another minute or two, then Ariel and Zach nearly knocked over their parents as they ran back to the stairs.

"Gonna check out the back yard," said Zach. He slowed to count the steps again. Ariel waited for him at the bottom before they raced to the back door.

"They seem pretty excited," said Kelly, who had followed them half the way up the stairs, clearly having given up on any kind of organized tour.

"Like kids in a candy store," said Ian. The smile he'd found upon discovering his office hadn't left his face. Lyana loved that smile.

After Lyana and Ian finished exploring the bedrooms and studying the overall layout of the second floor, they stared out the bay window to see the kids in the back yard and the creek beyond.

"Maybe we should follow their lead and head outside?" Ian said.

The property was hugged by trees, with a sprawling yard both in the front and the back of the house. English style gardens sat to the left, an old iron bench nestled at the edge of the water to the right, and what felt like miles of forest lay just beyond. Soothing whispers rustled through the leaves; the creek babbled its reply.

As Lyana watched the children laughing and running around the yard, an overwhelming sense of peace washed over her. She could breathe.

Ian put his arm around Lyana and pulled her close, then looked at Kelly. "We'll take it."

After allowing the kids a little more time to race around the yard, they gathered themselves and began to pile into the car for the trip back to the city. Ian climbed into the driver's seat. Lyana paused and looked at the house again, lost in the possibilities.

"I will get started on the paperwork right away," Kelly interrupted her reverie. "We can meet back at the office. You have the address?"

Lyana glanced into the car at Ian who nodded.

"We do."

"See you there, then."

Kelly walked away and Lyana slipped into her seat. Ian started the car. A moment later, Kelly had jogged back to the driver's side. She stood there, an expectant look on her face. Ian lowered the window. Her expression eased into one of those forced realtor smiles.

"I almost forgot. There's a caretaker who lives on the property. It's part of the deal, he comes with the house." She shrugged like it was no big deal.

Lyana's hopes fell.

The rollercoaster.

"What do you mean, it's part of the deal?" asked Ian. "Is he a tenant?"

"No, no. Not really, anyway. You own all the land but as part of Mr. Goodpasture's will, the property could only be sold on the condition his nephew kept a one-acre plot on the corner of the property." She pointed, but Lyana couldn't tell what she was pointing at. "He mostly keeps to himself, but he's also available to help with the property, if you like. He certainly knows its quirks. But you can see him as much or as little as you'd like."

Ian turned to look at Lyana. She gave him her best pleading look, but it wasn't necessary. Still looking into Lyana's eyes, he said, "I'm sure it will be fine. We probably *could* use some help with all this land." He reached over and placed his hand on Lyana's.

"I'm so glad to hear that," said Kelly. She stood there awkwardly for a moment, then hustled off to her car.

Ian rolled up the window and they followed Kelly down the driveway.

They had found their home.

FIVE

T HE LAST OF the boxes were almost unpacked.
Summer was coming to a close and the children
would soon start at their new school. The previous six
weeks were a blur of packing and making all the arrangements
for the move, followed by the unpacking of boxes as they
settled into their new home. Lyana could hardly believe it had
all been done, and with surprisingly little stress considering
Ian had spent most of those weeks traveling and lecturing
to promote his latest book.

There were moments when it still didn't feel real, even
though she saw all the empty boxes she had packed (and
unpacked) mostly by herself. But as Lyana stood in her new
kitchen, floors littered with the remnants of bubble wrap and
old newspapers, she was finally able to take a deep breath.

They had really done it. What seemed like a pipe dream
only months ago was now a reality. In the midst of all the
change, it was hard to stop and enjoy it with the mounting
to-do list, but as she grabbed her great grandmother's necklace in her hands, holding it tightly to her chest, she paused.

There was something familiar and yet stirring about
this place. As much as she wanted to keep her eyes focused
on the new life they would build here, she felt a pull that

kept bringing her back to everything she would have rather left behind.

She cried out "Stop!" to stay in the here and now, the word rolling off her tongue with nobody to receive it. She had everything she could have ever wanted right in front of her, they had all come so far to get to this place, the last thing she wanted to do was lose sight of that. The past still hurt too much.

She slowly opened her hands, looking down at the piece of jewelry that had served as a constant reminder of her history, and the family she left behind.

A faint whisper came from down the hall, too soft to make out any words.

Is someone here?

She hesitantly looked around the corner but saw no one.

But there it was again. This time, the voice whispered her name. *Lyana.*

Trying to follow the voice, she found herself in the empty pantry. Looking around the barren room, her heart began to race. As she caught a glimpse of herself in the pantry mirror, her grip loosed on the necklace. It slipped through her fingers as all the tension in her body released.

Everything went black.

Lyana is nine years old. Her parents have only recently divorced. A daddy's girl, Lyana reminds her mother so much of him that when he left, the bitterness and anger her mother felt toward him was redirected at her. She is on the receiving end of all the broken dreams and feels like everything is her fault. She knows deep down that it isn't. She has no control over him leaving, just as she can't control her mother's actions towards her.

There are moments she wishes he had taken her with him. *Why leave me here? With her!*

Lyana is in middle school now. She is a straight-A student, always responsible, a dedicated learner. She participates in after-school activities and is active in her church youth group. She took up music at a young age and shows so much promise. It is the one outlet she has away from it all, where she can just disappear for hours. Music makes sense in her painful world. So does her sincere, young faith. Those two things keep her grounded. But as much as she tries to be perfect, her efforts are never enough. She wants nothing more than to be seen and loved by her mother, but always falls short of her acceptance. It is a never-ending cycle.

She and her younger sister Eliza believed everything would change when their mother met Stan. It was a chance to start over and be a happy family again. Or at least a happier one. Instead, things only got worse. The yelling, the abuse. Everything bad that had ever happened to her mother is now being directed toward her. The very act of her breathing ignites a storm of rage. Now, she is not only the target of her mother's discontent, but a target for Stan's as well.

Because of Eliza's chronic health problems, Lyana has become her protector. She takes care of Eliza when her mother is preoccupied, something that's been happening a lot lately. She cooks for the two of them and makes sure Eliza is fed and kept safe. She knows if she doesn't take care of Eliza, it is likely she won't make it. Eliza's many surgeries and all that time spent in the hospital have left her both physically and mentally stunted. She is destined to spend the rest of her youth simply trying to catch up to others her own age. This prompts Lyana to take the brunt of Stan's abuse, intercepting anything targeting Eliza to keep her from further harm.

The first time Stan throws Lyana against the wall and pins her to the floor with his enormous body, it is like watching a movie in slow motion. She knows it is happening but feels like she is having an out of body experience. He is hovering over her, seething through his teeth like an enraged animal. This isn't supposed to be her life. She is the perfect student. The girl with so much promise. What has she done to deserve this? What is so wrong with her that her own mother won't even come to her defense? And why does she allow this to happen over and over again?

Lyana is seventeen years old. For seven years she has endured her mother's disappointment and Stan's physical outbursts, and each time the anger would swell inside her like a volcano on the brink of eruption.

She is so excited she can barely contain herself as her steps turn into a brisk run back to the house. Earlier that day, she learned she had been selected to participate in a songwriting competition. If she did well enough, she could qualify for the national competition and gain exposure that could literally change the course of her future.

She and her music instructor spent a few hours after school working on a new arrangement of a song she had been writing for months, and she is excited to show Eliza and her mother, even though she knows her mother isn't likely to offer the kind of reaction she longs for. For a split second, she has a glimmer of hope that maybe this will be the moment that softens her mother. But it is a fleeting thought, and she quickly lets it go. She knows from experience not to set herself up for that type of disappointment.

"Eliza! Eliza! You are never going to believe what happened today," she blurts out as she comes running into the house.

It is a modest house. White with dull red shutters. Single story. Three bedrooms. Two bathrooms. It hasn't been updated since the mid-Seventies. She runs through the living room and into the kitchen where Eliza is sitting at the table doing her homework.

Eliza's face lights up, but then just as quickly retreats to a cautious expression. She nods toward the living room, then shakes her head twice to signal to Lyana that the news will have to wait until the girls are alone. But Lyana doesn't catch Eliza's cues quickly enough and a squeal of excitement slips out of her mouth.

It's too late, Stan has heard them.

He storms into the kitchen like a raging bull, stopping just inches from Lyana's face.

"I told you kids that when I'm home I expect you to keep quiet!" he shouts. There are only shouts these days. Lyana steps in front of Eliza, who remains sitting at the table. Lyana's petite frame is all that is standing between her sister and her stepfather's six-foot, three-inch, muscular body.

"How many times do I have to tell you?!" His voice echoes off the walls and he lunges for Lyana. She can smell the alcohol on his breath as she cowers, using the sheets of music she has spent hours working on as a shield even though she knew they wouldn't protect her from his rage.

He grabs the song she's been working on, the song she is so proud of, from her hands and, just like the first time he pushed her all those years ago, she watches in slow motion as he rips her dream to shreds.

Satisfied with his destruction, he laughs and tosses the torn strips of paper at her feet.

"That'll teach you," he slurs. Then he stumbles away, back to his chair and the lukewarm beer that was likely waiting for him in his dark cave of a living room.

The girls quickly and quietly collect the pieces of torn paper, then Lyana takes Eliza by the hand and runs to the nearest place that feels safe. The pantry. They sneak inside and lock the door behind them.

Lyana falls to her knees sobbing, holding the shredded pieces of paper that only moments earlier represented hope and a chance to leave this place. Now, as she holds tightly to the jagged edges, they remind her instead of her broken family and all the hurt she has bottled up through the years. Like a puzzle she was never able to figure out. She could tape the pieces back together, but that would never erase what had just happened, what had been happening for years.

The sadness and anger are too much to bear.

She vows it will be the last time he hurts her.

"Mom, are you okay?"

Zach was standing in front of Lyana holding a glass of water, looking down at her with concern in his eyes. It was only then that she realized she was huddled on the floor in the corner of the pantry.

She picked herself up, brushed off imaginary dust and offered her best "everything is fine" smile. "I'm okay, Zach. I … I'm here. I was … I was just having a moment." Zach was a smart and observant kid. The concerned look in his eyes told her everything she needed to know. But a moment later, he shrugged, took a long sip of his water, then started to walk away.

She went back to collecting the pile of trash on the floor. Gathering it in her arms, she called out to Zach, "Come help me, this house isn't going to unpack itself!" He paused, then spun a perfect 180 degrees on one foot—which brought an awkward smile—then returned to the kitchen.

The two of them laughed as they worked together to clean up the mess. Time with her son served as a good distraction for Lyana. The haze of her unbidden memories quickly dissipated, and she returned fully to the present. She tossed an armful of bubble wrap in the air and she and Zach danced around it, laughing even harder.

There was freedom in her laughter. It had taken her years to learn to laugh again.

As she lay in bed later that night, Lyana paused, thinking back to the strange moment in the pantry, to the memory of that day when she was seventeen. It was like a magnet had pulled her back in time, forcing her to relive the emotions that consumed her. It was a day she would rather wipe from her memory altogether, one of so many days from her childhood. But that one was different. That one changed everything.

She reached across the bed to feel Ian next to her. His presence always calmed her restless thoughts. Her eyes closed, and she drifted off to sleep.

SIX

"MOM, HE'S DOING it again! Make him stop."

The house was abuzz with activity as Zach and Ariel were getting ready for the first day at their new school. They were running around putting last-minute items into their backpacks, grabbing something to eat for breakfast and trying to get it all done before it was time to go.

Lyana was making coffee when Zach ran into the kitchen.

"... 7, 8, 9 ..." Zach's voice trailed off.

"Tell him to knock it off," Ariel yelled as she followed Zach, shielding herself using the kitchen island. Zach lunged at her from the other side trying to grab the pencils she was holding. When he missed, she made a face at him and pleaded with her mother.

"He keeps doing it and it's so annoying!"

While she was distracted, Zach grabbed the pencils out of her hand and went back to packing his backpack.

"… 10, 11, 12. Perfect! All accounted for."

Ariel grabbed a granola bar and huffed off, shaking her head at her brother. "Are you sure you have all twelve?" she called back, a subtle sneer in her voice.

Zach looked troubled for a moment, but Lyana reassured him that he'd counted correctly. She was used to the two of them bickering at one another. They argued like most siblings do but had just as many moments being best friends, although the two of them couldn't be more different.

Ariel had always been outgoing and easily made friends. Like her mother, she had a captivating presence about her. She was always the center of attention with the popular crowd and was involved in as many activities as possible. Zach was more of a loner. He had always been unusually sensitive from the time he was a young boy. Lyana and Ian knew he was special.

They first noticed his unique behavioral tendencies the first time the family took a vacation to the beach. Most kids his age were running along the dunes, in and out of the water, accumulating sand between their toes, behind their knees, and anywhere else the tiny granules could find a home. But for two-year-old Zach, the gritty feeling was too overwhelming, and would send him into a state of panic. What started with sand, moved on to the seams of his socks, then loud noises in crowds. For him, those things were almost unbearable. While his intense sensitivities made him more in tune with the world around him and aware of the emotions of others, they ultimately left him isolated in most social situations. He ached to connect and fit in, but the more he tried, the more it seemed to push others away. He learned sooner than most that kids could be so cruel about things they just don't understand.

Making friends didn't come as naturally for Zach as it did Ariel, but Lyana was hopeful that a new school would open opportunities for him to start fresh, meet new people, and make new friends.

Ian emerged from the study and greeted Lyana, pouring his coffee into his favorite rocket ship travel mug.

"Five-minute warning," he said. Ian was the designated driver for school drop-offs.

Zach and Ariel grabbed their backpacks, making a mad dash around the house to ensure they didn't forget anything, then raced to the bathroom to brush their teeth after being reminded of that morning ritual for the hundredth time.

Lyana followed Ian and the kids to the garage. Zach looked back and quickly returned to his mother for one last hug, apprehension and excitement battling for prominence on his face. Ariel, bold and brave as usual, waved and yelled out, "Love you, Mom!" as she pounced into the front passenger seat, "Shot gun!"

Lyana stood in the doorway, watching with more than a hint of anxiety as they pulled away.

She shut the door behind her and turned back to the kitchen. Slowly sipping her coffee in the stillness of her new home, she let out a deep breath and leaned on the island her children had just been fighting over. Her serene view out the bay window in the breakfast nook overlooked the expansive front yard. The morning dew twinkled on the grass. She squinted at the sunlight reflecting off the car windows as Ian and the kids drove away.

Please let today go well for them.

Realizing she had forgotten to have breakfast, she scoured the pantry for something to eat. As she reached for the box of Strawberry Pop-Tarts, she paused to look at herself in the old, weathered mirror that hung on the pantry wall. She studied the lines on her face, then watched them slowly fade away. As the years began to vanish, once more she felt an unsettling tug toward the mirror as the image of her kitchen in the background disappeared.

She blinked.

Lyana is seventeen again. The pantry surrounding her is stale and lifeless. Years of use have scuffed the fading white paint and left several of the wire shelving units crooked. This tiny room holds all the secrets and shame that she has known. Her infinite tangle of bottled-up emotions could more than fill the mostly-empty shelves.

She glances in the mirror at the kitchen behind her. The once pale walls are bright, new, as if they've just been painted. Custom wood cabinets call to her with the promise of white plates and cobalt blue glasses and laughter-fueled family dinners. The drop lighting hanging above the glass cabinet doors bounces off gold cabinet hardware. The stained white tile floor, the place where she has spent so many moments curled up crying, morphs into a stunning black and white checkered pattern. As she looks up, the popcorn ceiling that reminds her of a bad art project turns into magnificent, aged tin square panels displaying an ornate fleur-de-lis pattern.

It is beautiful in every possible way. She reaches out to touch the mirror …

Lyana looked at her hands. She was holding the box of Strawberry Pop-Tarts. She glanced at the old mirror that they'd half-considered removing from the pantry and was puzzled by what she saw. The kitchen was just as it had been since the day they'd arrived. And her face—her face looked tired. She tried to shake off the strange feeling that lingered in the periphery of her brain.

"It must be exhaustion," she said aloud to her reflection.

She took a deep breath and thought about what she'd just experienced. The more she sat with it, the clearer everything became. The vision was so detailed and breathtaking, the complete opposite of the home she grew up in.

And just like that, she knew exactly what to do.

SEVEN

A S THE SCHOOL buses passed by the diner window, Lloyd Warner glanced over at his patrons sipping their coffee, some of them parents of school-age children. The smiles on their faces meant summer was coming to an end. The community pool would be closing soon, and all the adventures that begin with kids riding their bikes would be put on hold until next June. As in other small towns, the locals readily celebrated the first day of school each year as it marked life returning to a predictable normal.

"Did you hear someone bought the Goodpasture place?" Toby Williams' deep voice was unmistakable.

The table reserved for the morning coffee crew sat at the front of the café in the corner by the window. Toby was one of about ten regulars who had been coming there for years, filling the chairs at that table every morning like clockwork. On any given day, at least five of them would show up. On a good day, all of them. Most would sit there for hours, sipping coffee, getting refills, sipping more coffee, and talking about everything and nothing. But the few who weren't yet retired would make their way to work after a quick catch up once the buses passed.

"That must have taken an act of God," said Harold Powers. That brought a few chuckles.

"Nah, just an act of Kelly," said Toby.

The chuckles turned to a roar of laughter. Lloyd made his way over to see what all the fuss was about.

"Pull up a chair, Lloyd. We're just chatting about Farr Hill," said Harold.

"What do you know about the new family who moved in?" asked Wayne Lewis, the youngest member of the group. He was one of only two who still had school-age children.

Lloyd was cautious about what he contributed to conversations or rumblings around town. After all, his business was built on being a place where people could come and just be themselves. Besides, gossip wasn't in his DNA.

"A family from Boston. Mom and dad, two kids," he said nonchalantly, signaling that was the extent of what he knew.

"Anyone want to place bets on how long they stay?" asked Harold. This sparked another round of roaring laughter.

"Maybe this time it will be different," offered Lloyd. "Maybe Farr Hill is just what this family has been looking for." He smiled at the group. "Who needs another cup?"

Several people pushed their cups forward, signaling an agreeable yes to another cup, while Wayne got up from the table.

"It's about that time. I better get to it," said Wayne.

As he walked out the door, Lloyd's attention turned from pouring more coffee to the woman coming through the door. He hadn't seen her before. Chances were none of the regulars had either.

Dave Cristian, the white-haired, Santa-bearded longest standing member of the morning coffee crew, with his mouth full of day old and slightly crunchy coffee cake, pointed not too discretely, and mouthed to Lloyd, "Who's that?"

Lloyd shrugged and made his way to the front counter.

"What suits you?" he asked as he slipped in behind the display case.

"Hi, I'm not really looking for coffee today … I'm looking for the hardware store. I'm new to the area."

The woman offered a pleasant, if somewhat embarrassed smile and Lloyd returned a sincere one.

"If you go left from here, then take another left at Meadows, you're almost there." Lloyd wondered if this might be the mom who moved into Farr Hill. If so, that would be quite the coincidence. "It's no more than a ten-minute walk or a two-minute drive."

"Thank you. I appreciate it." She eyed the pastries in the display case. "Those look delicious," she said.

"Made fresh daily," said Lloyd. Someone in the coffee group stifled a laugh. "Mostly anyway," Lloyd added, offering a scowl to the peanut gallery. "You said you're new to the area. Where are you from?"

"My family just moved here from Boston." She extended her hand. "I'm Lyana Keane."

Lloyd put down the pot of coffee he was still holding and wiped his hand on his apron, then extended it. "Lloyd Warner. I own this joint," he said with a smile.

"Nice to meet you, Lloyd." She smiled. "I'll definitely have to come back soon for one of those fresh daily, mostly anyway, pastries."

This made Lloyd's smile even bigger. He liked this newcomer.

"Please do. We also serve up a mean breakfast."

"Gotta love a mean breakfast. I'll be back. Thanks again!"

She opened the door, triggering the bell, then headed left outside the shop. When she finally disappeared from view, Toby called Lloyd over to the table.

"Who was that?" he asked.

"Looks like that is Lyana Keane from Boston."

"The Goodpasture house?"

"Seems so."

Lloyd went back to wiping the counter and cleaning up from the breakfast rush. The regulars returned to their conversation, chatting away about whatever it was that captured their interest. That subject, unsurprisingly, was the new family at Farr Hill.

"I wonder if they have met *him* yet." Jim prodded. He was looking right at Lloyd, probably hoping he knew.

Lloyd opened his mouth to reply, then thought better of it. When no one offered an answer, the conversation was quickly displaced by talk about the new high school football coach.

Lloyd wasn't thinking about the coach. He was still pondering Jim's question.

EIGHT

AS IAN PULLED into the garage, having spent the last several minutes listening to Zach and Ariel recount their first day at school, he decided to offer a gentle warning.

"Your mother has been at it again," he said.

Ariel and Zach's smiles disappeared in unison.

"What do you mean?" asked Zach, concern obvious in his voice.

"No, it's not … I mean, it's not a bad thing. She's just … on a mission."

Ariel huffed. "What is it this time? Arranging books by the color of their spine?"

"No," said Ian, though he wouldn't put it past Lyana, considering the unexpected nature of her recent behavior.

The kids didn't wait for further explanation. Even before the car was put in park, curiosity got the best of them and they threw open the doors and ran into the house to see what was going on. Ian followed close behind.

"Mom?" Zach said, both a statement and a question. She turned to look up at Ian, then the kids, who stood there wide-eyed, staring at the torn-apart pantry, at their mother wearing old clothes and holding a paintbrush.

"Hey, guys! How was the first day of school?" Lyana swiped the back of her hand across her forehead, leaving a thin stripe of white paint behind.

"So …?" Ariel began, then lifted her hands in a "what's all this?" gesture.

"I'm renovating the pantry. I got inspired this morning. Something just came over me and I wanted to get started right away. It's a little hard to explain, but let's just say it's time for a change."

The two kids chimed in with a hesitant, "Umm … okay then."

"Told you she's been busy," said Ian. He wondered if they were going to ask more questions, but hunger pangs outweighed their curiosity as they searched for snacks through the food that should have been in the pantry but was stacked on the counter. Not a moment later, they found what they were looking for and scooted off to head upstairs to their rooms.

"All good?" Ian had spent much of the day watching Lyana fervently rush around looking for supplies. He was glad she had found something to be excited about but recognized the signs. This was clearly another manic episode. He couldn't shake the feeling that something sinister was driving her sudden "inspiration" this time.

"I am so excited. This is going to be amazing," she said. She turned to look at the pantry. It wasn't anywhere close to amazing yet, but once Lyana put her mind to something, there was no stopping her. She had always been single-minded about tasks. Usually, that was a gift–she got things done, and efficiently. This time, Ian wasn't so sure.

He considered saying something about the paint on her face, then stopped. She wouldn't care anyway, at least not until she had finished the day's work. "Let me know if you need anything," he said instead.

"I will."

"I'm going to see if Zach wants to go exploring outside."

"Okay," Lyana responded without turning around. "Have fun."

Ian watched her for a minute before leaving the kitchen. She was intensely focused on her task but didn't seem stressed or troubled by it. With every stroke of her paintbrush, she settled into a calming rhythm.

He shrugged. Maybe this was just what it looked like—a simple home improvement project.

Ian wanted to believe that, but his gut told him it wasn't so simple.

NINE

NOT REALIZING JUST how vast their new property was, the father and son duo lost track of time exploring outside.

As the minutes turned into hours, Ian noticed a haze lingering at the edge of the trees, much like that first day they came to see the house.

"Dad, did you know that fog consists of tiny water droplets and ice crystals suspended in the air near the Earth's surface?" Ian's attention turned from the layer of fog to Zach's explanation of it. "It is like a cloud touching the ground. There are four different types."

Ian was impressed that Zach knew so much about fog, but he wasn't surprised in the least. Zach was an information sponge.

"The foggiest city in the world is actually New Orleans," he continued. "And did you know fog has played a part in many historic battles, too?"

"No, I didn't know that. But … speaking of fog …" began Ian.

"Is this going to be one of those lame dad jokes?" Zach interrupted.

"No, no. Not this time." Ian stopped walking and Zach nearly ran into him. "I was just going to say that my brain has been a little foggy ever since I got back from the last conference. I got something for you, as always." Ian paused, watching Zach's expression morph from confusion to curiosity, then reached into his pocket and pulled out a woven leather bracelet with a stone attached to it. Zach held out his hand and Ian dropped it into his eager fingers. Zach turned the bracelet over in his hands and looked closely at the stone.

"This is so cool!" he said, slipping the bracelet on his wrist. It was a little big, but Zach didn't seem to mind. "What's this symbol?" he asked, pointing to the image carved into the stone.

"That's called an ouroboros," said Ian.

"It looks like a snake eating its tail." Zach traced the intricate circular image with his right index finger.

"That's exactly what an ouroboros is," said Ian.

"It's like infinity," said Zach, mesmerized by the gift. "I love it."

They started walking again. Ian was pleased by how much Zach liked the gift. He always brought gifts to the kids after his trips. He welcomed the challenge of finding something unique to surprise them with every time.

After a rare moment of silence, Zach began posing questions about infinity. They both loved talking about impossible things and Zach was an expert at asking big questions. Just as Ian was about to respond to Zach, he tripped over something, lost his balance, and fell to the ground.

"I'm fine," he said before Zach could express his concern. But Zach wasn't looking at him. He was looking at the ground in front of him.

Ian stood up and brushed the dirt from his knees and followed Zach's gaze.

"Dad what is that?" Zach asked.

The two began to remove the brush and leaves that had gathered on what, upon closer inspection, appeared to be a door. A door in the dirt.

It was a door, framed by crumbling concrete, but to *what*? A cellar? A shelter?

Ian was fascinated by the oversized, rusting hinges that were decorated with what looked like a Celtic symbol.

No, much earlier. Different culture. Maybe Sumerian?

He leaned in to explore further.

"Dad, help me with this."

Ian looked at Zach, who was tugging at the door's old iron handle. He stepped over and helped Zach pull on it. At first, the door didn't budge, and Ian thought it might be sealed shut. But then it moved. They pulled harder and the door moved even more. It was heavy—much heavier than Ian would have guessed. With each attempt, Ian's imagination ran wild with ideas of what might lurk beyond.

"Well, hello," a voice said from behind them.

Startled, Ian and Zach dropped the door with a loud bang and turned in surprise.

Ian studied the man. He appeared to be in his fifties and stood about five feet, nine inches tall. The years had been kind to the stranger. He was neither overweight nor frail—probably an athlete in his younger days, thought Ian. His dark hair had begun to recede, and the greys showed ever so slightly through the remaining hair on his head and the unshaven scruff on his chin and jawline. He was unassuming, dressed in workman's overalls and steel toe boots. His dark eyes, however, had a gripping intensity—they instantly pierced into Ian's thoughts. Looking into them was like seeing the experiences of his life reflecting back at you. And yet there was a quiet confidence in his demeanor that eased Ian's quickening heart.

"I'm Marshall," the man said. Ian was trying to recall the name. "The Caretaker," he added.

"That's right. I completely forgot." Ian had wondered, when they closed on the house, when they might run into the caretaker, but then had nearly forgotten about him in the time since.

Zach was squinting, carefully studying Marshall.

"I'm Ian Keene. And this is my son, Zach."

Zach continued to stare at the man, not unkindly, but wearing a curious expression.

Marshall nodded. "Are you fellas a bit lost?"

Ian shook his head. "We were just out getting a feel for the property. This is an amazing place."

Zach interrupted his dad with a list of burning questions. "Have you been here long? What is this door all about? Did you know the previous family that lived here? Do you have any kids? Have you …"

"Whoa, bud, slow down!"

Marshall's expression didn't change. Ian couldn't tell if he was bothered or tickled by Zach's curiosity. "I've been here as long as I can remember," he replied. He didn't bother to answer the other questions.

The light of day was starting to fade as the three stood at the mysterious door. Ian was about to press for more information about the door when Zach spoke up.

"Uh … Dad, we should get back."

Ian recognized Zach's tone. It wasn't one of fearfulness—Marshall seemed like a harmless enough man—but one of slowly building anxiety. The sky was darkening, after all. Their explorations had simply left them without a concept of time.

Marshall nodded, looked over at Zach. "You two really should hurry along before …" He froze. It was almost as if he'd seen a ghost. The sudden change in Marshall's demeanor unnerved Ian, but it was short-lived. Marshall continued, "Before it gets too dark. You wouldn't want to get lost in this forest." Marshall had positioned himself in front of the cellar door, a subtle signal that their explorations had come to an end for the day. "I'll be happy to show you around the property another time."

"We just might take you up on that," said Ian. "It was a pleasure meeting you, Marshall. Come on, Zach." Zach stared a beat longer at Marshall, then focused back the way they'd come.

As the two of them walked away, Zach glanced back toward Marshall.

"He's already gone," said Zach.

Ian turned to see that Zach was right. Marshall had left just as quickly as he had appeared.

Zach turned his focus back to his father. "Well, that was weird."

"Yeah, you think?"

The two of them talked about meeting Marshall and laughed about how they had completely forgotten someone else lived on the property. They couldn't believe how quickly time had passed during their adventures.

As they approached the house, Zach ran on ahead, clearly eager to share their adventure with his mother and show her his new bracelet. Ian walked in as Zach was excitedly talking about the door in the dirt.

Lyana stood up and swiped at her face, brushing the hair back from her eyes and smearing paint near her eyebrow. Her face and hands had more than a few splotches of paint now. She'd clearly been hard at work while they were away. Ariel came running down the stairs to see what all the commotion was about.

"You found what?" asked Lyana.

"Dad and I found an old cellar door in the woods, and then we met Marshall."

"Marshall?"

The look on Lyana's face told Ian that she had forgotten as well. He laughed and said with a smile, "The Caretaker!"

"Oh, of course! I'd forgotten about him."

Lyana's face suddenly went white. She looked over at the stove, then the refrigerator.

"I'm sorry, I totally lost track of time. I don't have a dinner plan."

Ian already had his phone out. "No worries. I just found a pizza place that looks promising," he said.

Later, their appetites sated, Ian took in the scene before him at the kitchen table. Their stories had painted the house with joy. It practically glowed from the roars of laughter, the energy of its new residents bringing it to life again.

Still, two stray thoughts threatened to distract him from that joy. What had spooked Marshall? And why did the man seem familiar?

Ian shook the thoughts from his head. Surely it was nothing.

• • •

Marshall slipped amongst the trees to watch Ian and Zach head back to the house. When young Zach turned around to look for him, Marshall shook his head. *This is an unexpected twist*, he thought.

When the two finally disappeared into the distance, a sudden breeze picked up and swirled the leaves into a ground tornado, conveniently covering the cellar door once again. Marshall glanced up into the trees and shook his head again, allowing a half-smile creeping onto his face.

A few moments later, a puzzled Marshall walked through the front door of his rustic cabin, closing the creaking door behind him. The late evening sun trickled in through the singular window, painting the wooden floor in patches of fading amber light. Marshall went to the bookshelf and scanned it, making sure everything was in its place. It was, and that confounded Marshall even more.

He stepped over to his table and scraped a match against the textured surface, then lit the antique lantern that sat there. The smell of kerosene filled the small room. It was a reassuring smell for Marshall. A comforting smell. He desperately needed something comforting in that moment.

He sat and picked up a half-finished carving of a ram. He turned it around in his hand, briefly admiring his own craftsmanship, then set it back down on the table. He glanced around the room as he had done so many times before, entranced by the dancing shadows. He was familiar with shadowy places, having spent so much time in them.

Like in the wings of an auditorium.

Marshall's eyes grew heavy.

He scooted the chair back, stood, pulled the curtain across the window, then shuffled over to his bed and lay down. The flame from the lamp continued to flicker as he lay there, exhausted.

TEN

*A*T TIMES, LIFE *moves so quickly he can barely remember the last week, while at other times it drags like molasses. He feels a constant aching pain in his heart, often questioning what has become of him. Will this life be all he knows? When will it be time?*

When he purchased the piece of land just outside Littleton, he knew it was the beginning of the end; the house would be symbolic of that. The life he had led, the places he had seen, the adventures he had experienced, and lessons he had learned. The lingering sting of losing loved ones.

Losing her.

His weathered hands grip a sketch. She was the love of his life. It feels like just yesterday, but he knows many years have passed and still, a day doesn't go by that he doesn't think of her. From the first moment he saw her, he knew. She was breathtaking and kind, full of life. She was the only family he had ever known. From the time he was a young boy, she was his home.

He stands, looking at the stone foundation. It is nearly ready. Surrounded by trees blowing ever so slightly in the wind, the water flows over and around the rocks in the creek. It is peaceful—the very solitude he is looking for. The house is for her. He will build it with his own hands, creating a masterpiece in her honor. It will hold all the memories of their past, the places they had seen together, the things he had collected through the years in his attempt to fix it all.

It will be where he waits ... for the end.

He returns the sketch in his jacket pocket, next to his heart, where he has kept it for years. As he tucks her away, he reaches into the pocket of his slacks and pulls out a broken stone. He grips it tightly and walks across the foundation. The vibrant stone radiates flecks of blue, green, and yellow, with a dominant blazing of red against the black background. When it is held to the light, it glows like frozen fire. One end is smooth and perfectly polished and the other is jagged and rough to the touch. He takes one final look at it and kneels, placing it directly in the center of the foundation where the house will soon stand.

Brick by brick and beam by beam he builds for years. He wants every detail to be perfect. He hires locals to help lift the timber frame and install the chimney, before adding the stairs and support beams. It is an immense undertaking and word about the unique home being built outside Littleton spreads quickly through the neighboring towns. People speak about its beauty and splendor. It is grand. Like nothing they have seen before.

As he works, he often hears cars nearing on the driveway, coming to take a peek. He enjoys the privacy the long driveway affords him and wants to maintain that, so he adds an iron gate at the clearing, deterring guests from arriving unannounced. They can still see the house from the barrier, but it keeps them from getting too close.

He pours everything he has into the house.

Everything.

ELEVEN

AS THE PAGES of the calendar turned, the changing leaves created a magnificent tapestry of colors lining the streets of the town and hillside. Farr Hill was a breathtaking patchwork of yellow, orange, and red. The whisper of fog was a seemingly permanent fixture on the property where mornings featured sunbursts peeking out amongst the colorful trees, accompanied by the redolent scent of the soil reclaiming the fallen leaves. It was quite the departure from their previous life of skyscrapers and traffic jams and exhaust fumes, but they were all settling into their new surroundings with ease.

Lyana was nearly done with the pantry remodel. For the rest of the family, the mess was an inconvenience but for her it was a welcome distraction from the pain she was still carrying. It was breathing life into her. Most mornings after everyone had left the house, she would take a moment to reflect and give gratitude for the life they were living, but some days her heart raced with anxiety and her mind spun with chaotic thoughts. She felt a sense of urgency that there was more to all of this—that this was much more than just a pantry remodel.

What am I doing? Why am I so driven? Why is this so important?

Lyana began to fade away into her thoughts but was startled back to reality by a sound coming from the kitchen. She looked up, confused.

"Ian?" she called out.

When there was no answer, she peeked her head around the corner. The kitchen was empty and she found nothing amiss, so she went back to focusing on her work in the pantry.

• • •

As Ian stared at the books that lined the walls of his office, waiting for a moment of inspiration to fill the blank screen staring back at him, his thoughts began to wander.

For Ian, this move had come with significant changes. He walked away from a full class schedule and long list of research projects. He had considered early retirement and was even offered emeritus status but chose instead to teach a few courses online. His new part-time status allowed for more focus on other projects. Like perhaps starting the next book he had begun to envision over the past year.

Ian's love for history started as a young boy. Some people have numerous interests and career paths over the years, but not Ian Keane. As a boy in a small Kentucky town, he could be found on most days with his head buried deep in a history book. It started with this fascination of his mother's home in Ireland, about his ancestry, and morphed into a passion from there. He couldn't get enough.

Much like Lyana, he never quite felt like he fit in. She was the dark-skinned girl from the other side of the tracks. He was the boy with the foreign-born mother. The two became friends as eight-year-olds, and were like two peas in a pod from that point forward. Their friendship carried them through some of the most difficult times growing up; from Lyana's parents' divorce and all she endured with her mother and stepfather, to Ian's own childhood chaos at the hands of the adults in his life.

His parents had met in a whirlwind, the Kentucky cowboy and the proper Irish girl. She was visiting the States when they met, and it all happened so quickly. She was his fourth wife. Not even a year later, Ian was born. His father was a known womanizer, a revolving door for questionable relationships, and as often drunk as not. He was as irresponsible with his children as he was with the women he charmed, then dumped. And he was an extremely violent man. Ian grew up in a house fraught with abuse, often accompanying his bloodied mother to the hospital.

It was in those hospital rooms, while watching his bruised and broken mother recover from her latest injuries, that his love for books and reading began. As the hours and days passed, he read all about foreign worlds and different times— about the great explorers who had come before.

History was not only his passion but his escape. It was the outlet that allowed him and Lyana to leave Kentucky together.

The night she ran away from home, she showed up on his doorstep in tears, retelling the events of earlier in the evening. That night, the two talked about the life they wanted to create for themselves. Ian wanted to study at Boston University. Berklee College of Music was only a few miles away. The two devised a plan to leave for Boston as soon as they graduated.

As soon as they flipped their tassels, they packed up their beat-up Chevy Blazer and headed East. Before Lyana could even finish buckling her seat belt, Ian had already turned on the radio, singing along with The Carpenters as they merged onto the freeway toward a new chapter.

> *Before the risin' sun, we fly*
> *So many roads to choose*
> *We'll start out walkin' and learn to run*
> *And yes, we've just begun*

Ian vowed to never be like his father. And he kept that vow. He was a brilliant student whose desire to succeed and provide for his family led to several degrees and a tenure as a distinguished professor.

As he looked again at his bookshelf, his eyes began to drift. On the wall behind his desk, just above the amber bottle of Teeling Whiskey he'd been given as a going away present from his fellow professors, was a piece Lyana had gotten for him the year he received his master's degree. It was a framed Persian proverb that read: *History is a mirror of the past, and a lesson for the present.*

Ian took a deep breath, then exhaled, settling back into his chair. This was the first time since they moved that he had gotten a chance to focus on his latest book. But writing a book, he had painstakingly learned, was as much about overcoming all the distractions that cried out for attention as putting words on the page. He decided to lean into those distractions and consider the intricacies of the house. Perhaps he could find inspiration there. It was clearly a unique and special home, but it wasn't until he was sitting there looking around that he began to notice aspects of the house that seemed historically significant, like something he had read about or researched but couldn't place to a specific thing or time.

Lyana popped into the study, interrupting his meandering thoughts.

"Ian, why don't you take a break from writing and come enjoy a cup of coffee with me? I could use a bit of a break myself."

Ian looked back at the blank screen, then nodded.

"Good idea."

The two of them had come to enjoy their mornings wrapped in a blanket, sipping coffee on the bench in the back yard but would sometimes switch things up and sit at the bistro table nestled near the rose bush that was on the side of the house. The small patio was perfect for the bistro set the two of them had purchased early on in their marriage. It was one of those pieces they had considered getting rid of for years, but each time they tried, one of them couldn't bring themselves to let it go. That table and chairs signified something more for both of them.

In between sips of his coffee, Ian began humming ever so softly and gazed at Lyana. As she had a hundred times before, Lyana joined him, softly singing along under her breath.

Talkin' it over, just the two of us
Workin' together day to day
Together
Together

TWELVE

I T WAS 1997. Ian had just finished his master's thesis and would be starting full time as a professor working toward his PhD the following semester. He had been putting in so many hours studying and researching. This was the next step toward his goal. It was a goal Lyana believed in, too. Ian's sole reason for working so hard was to provide for his family in a way his father never had. Now that he was a father, that was even more important. He didn't need to say it, though—to Lyana, his intentions were clear: everything he did would be for the betterment of his family. He wanted to be the protector and provider he never had.

While Ian was laser-focused on the legacy he would create for the family, Lyana was balancing caring for their two small children and trying to get her music career off the ground. As much as she loved music, she knew that would eventually take a backseat to mothering her children—this was expected of her, just as it was of the many generations of women before her. There was an unspoken tradition in her culture for women to put their children first. It wasn't exactly easy for Lyana to embrace this tradition—music is what had saved her—but she knew it was the right choice.

They married at nineteen and became parents at twenty-one. There were three years between Ariel and Zach, and it was during those years that Lyana realized she had absolutely no idea what she was doing. A miscarriage at seventeen weeks during that interim was crushing for both Ian and Lyana, but not knowing how to talk about it, they buried it deep, longing to forget the pain and loss. Through the years, she often found herself wondering what life would be like with all three of their children—families of five would pass by on the street or she would catch a glimpse of them across a crowded restaurant, but the thoughts were too much to bear. She knew Ian felt the same deep pain. The loss of their child had changed them forever.

Of course, she was doing her best, but it didn't come naturally for her. She had never known unconditional love as a child, and now she was trying to figure out how to give that to these two small humans. While it stirred from within and she desperately wanted to be that nurturer for her children and her family, it was difficult and brought up so much that lurked beneath the surface—the pain, the anger.

Having kids was like facing the hurt she had been running from for all those years, and the anger reminded her of … her own mother. It was in those moments, when fighting with Ian or struggling with feelings of inadequacy as a parent, that she realized she needed to be better. She needed to be the change, to break the patterns that would plague her children and generations to come if she didn't do anything about it. But the anger had such a grip she didn't know how to change, how to become better. It was a losing battle in her mind.

If there was one thing she and Ian swore, it was that they would break the cycle of bad parenting they had both experienced. They did their best, but those years were extremely difficult with all the baggage they carried.

Like many young couples, the Keanes fought about finances and the division of labor, trying to find balance amid impossible schedules and the myriad demands of small children. Providing for his family was everything to Ian, but the self-inflicted pressure began to weigh heavily on him as he spent more time away from the kids on research trips and speaking engagements. In some ways he knew he was creating a better life for them, but in other ways he felt like they no longer needed him. The lack of connection with his family and doubts about his ability to be a good father caused Ian to turn to alcohol to numb the pain and loneliness.

Meanwhile, Lyana felt like she was the one sacrificing everything for the family. With Ian gone so often and emotionally disconnected, she often parented alone. Not surprisingly, this built resentment toward Ian. It was a quiet resentment at first—Lyana wanted desperately to do the right thing for her family. But then, one day, it wasn't so quiet anymore.

That's the thing with anger. It can only remain hidden for so long.

It all came to a head one afternoon as Lyana waited at home for Ian. And waited. And waited. She was exhausted, having spent the day caring for the kids by herself, but was looking forward to taking part in a writing session with a few songwriter friends who had been commissioned to create a song for the Boston Symphony, which was planning a James Taylor tribute. "Songwriter" was the one role Lyana had apart from being someone's mom or wife, and she needed it even more than she knew. So, when Ian finally called with slurred words to say he wouldn't be home until even later, all hell broke loose. He explained that he was in the middle of research when he got pulled into a meeting. That meeting then led to discussions with the Department Chair in the pub across the street from the university, and he just simply lost track of time. He told her it was an honest mistake, but Lyana felt betrayed and devalued by the one person who vowed to be there for her. Ian knew how important this night was for her.

How can he do this to me? I have to give music up, too?

Lyana hung up with Ian and called Eliza, who was now living in South Carolina. The floodgates ruptured, opening decades of pent-up emotions. All the years of feeling unseen, under-appreciated, or unloved by her family spilled out.

I just can't. I can't do this anymore.

She packed up the kids and didn't call Ian until after the car was ready to go.

"We'll be staying with my sister. I just ... I need space. From this marriage. From you and your ... your questionable choices. From everything," she said.

She learned later that those words broke Ian, bringing him to his knees. He had spent all these years pouring into his career as an act of love for his family, not realizing it was having the exact opposite effect on his wife. What he thought was a loving gesture left Lyana feeling lost and alone, secondary to his career and everything else in his life.

But in his own moment of anger, spurred on by lowered inhibitions thanks to more than a just a sip of usquebaugh, he told her to go, then hung up.

As she looked in the rearview mirror at her children, thinking she was walking away from hurt and anger, she had no idea how the trip ahead was about to change her heart.

The three of them stayed at a hotel near Baltimore that night. It was the first time Lyana and Ian had let an evening go by without speaking. Even when one or both of them had traveled before, they always made a point to connect on the phone before the end of the day.

Not that night.

The drive from Boston to Charleston took a few days, and as each day ended, neither Lyana nor Ian were ready to break the uncomfortable silence.

It was the first time for either of them that the pain from their childhood had caught up with them. They had done such a great job of supporting one another through all those hard moments when they were kids, but as young adults trying to make it work, they simply didn't know how.

Lyana had been in South Carolina with her sister for just over a week when Eliza offered to watch the kids so she could go for a stroll along the beach to clear her head. The salt air and sea breeze always had a way of making Lyana feel calm and centered.

She cupped her knees as she sat on the beach, her toes digging deeper into the sand in front of her. She closed her eyes to listen to the crashing waves. As the peace of that moment washed over her, tears began to roll down her cheeks. She was interrupted by a man calling out for his dog along the shore.

She turned her head toward the sound of his voice and her eyes locked with a weathered older man with a scruffy grey beard and a faded fisherman's cap.

"Sorry to interrupt Miss, but I'm looking for my dog. She's about yea high with black and white markings, answers to Anani. Have you seen her?" He paused for a moment, then concern etched his face. "Are you okay?" he asked.

Lyana nodded before bursting into uncontrollable sobs. The man sat down beside her and offered a shoulder for her to cry on. As she sat there with this stranger, she saw so clearly the moments of disappointment through the years and how they were bleeding into her own family. She saw the abuse she'd experienced, and the anger she felt toward her mother. The pain, the disappointment. The hurt. All the pieces of the past she was holding onto. There, sitting next to a stranger on the beach, she found herself face to face with all of it.

"Please help me. I can't do this anymore. I surrender! The words rolled off her tongue, even surprising herself.

Wait … what am I doing? I don't even know this man.

She quickly tried to gain her composure, pushing herself off his shoulder and wiping her face with her sleeve.

"I'm so sorry. I shouldn't have done that."

"That's okay, Miss. I've been around this sun more times than you could imagine, and I've seen a few things. Believe it or not, this isn't the first time this has happened to me, and I certainly don't expect it to be the last," he said with a wink and a gentle smile. Something about his demeaner and the softness in his eyes eased Lyana's mind.

She took a deep breath and opened her mouth to speak, but the words wouldn't come. For the first time in a long time, she felt seen and not alone.

"I don't know what you are going through," the stranger started, filling the awkward silence, "but I do know that life can come with a lot of pain. Letting go is very difficult, but I have learned in my long life that it's only when you let go that the healing comes. *There is much hope in hopelessness; for at the end of the dark night, there is light.*"

There was no way he could have known. Those were the same words her grandmother had spoken over her. It was an old Persian proverb; one she had passed down along with her necklace to Lyana when she was a young woman.

In that moment there on the beach, Lyana felt connected to something greater than herself. She knew then she wanted to live a life grounded in freedom from the past.

She determined to let it all go. Everything she had bottled up for years, the anger and the hurt. She accepted her part in all of it and vowed to break the chains around her heart. The moment felt bigger than she, orchestrated and out of her hands.

Life-changing.

Thunder rolled as the dark clouds moved in. Lyana heard a faint bark in the distance. The old man called for Anani and she came toward them, splashing in the waves running along the beach as fast as she could. She had found her own adventure amongst the sand dunes and beach shrubs.

"I wish you all the best," the man said as he stood. When he tipped his hat, she noticed an unusual tattoo on his left hand. She was only able to see a small portion peeking out from behind his coat sleeve and tried not to stare, but it reminded her of something she had seen before. His hand lowered as he turned and walked to his dog.

Lyana picked herself up from the sand and couldn't get back to Eliza's fast enough. The weight of her past was finally gone, and the only person she wanted to speak with was Ian.

When the two finally spoke, it was the most vulnerable they had been with one another. They opened up about all the ways in which they were holding back in life and marriage, afraid that if they allowed themselves to be truly happy and build a foundation of love that it would all be taken away. The thought had been too much for either of them, and both retreated into their own version of safety. For Lyana, that meant sitting with her anger and allowing resentment to control her life. For Ian, that meant pouring himself into his career and avoiding conflict. As the truth poured out, they promised to do better, to be more honest, to build the life they always imagined, to create something better and change the course for their own children.

Lyana hoisted the last suitcase into the trunk. She hugged her sister in a lingering embrace.

"Thank you for having us these past few weeks. I still don't know how, but I just know things will be different this time."

As she pulled out of the driveway, watching Eliza wave in the rear-view mirror, her thoughts turned toward seeing Ian again and their fresh start. Both kids fell asleep within minutes, exhausted as they were from the past few weeks of non-stop play with their cousins. She turned on the radio and settled in for the long drive. Lyana couldn't help but smile as a familiar voice rang out.

And when the evening comes, we smile
So much of life ahead
We'll find a place where there's room to grow
And yes, we've just begun

The time spent apart was exactly what they needed and set their family on an entirely new path of togetherness, openness, and healing. It was hard work, but with the help of an amazing counselor, there was joy in their home, a wholeness that neither of them had felt before. Ian was more intentional about finding the balance between work and family, always putting family first. Lyana spent time each morning in silent reflection and meditation, starting each day centered and at peace. She learned to let go and live one moment at a time.

The two wanted a spot to celebrate those moments together, so they replaced the tattered lawn chairs that had sat on the balcony since the day they moved in with the bistro table they picked out together. It wasn't extravagant, but it was all theirs.

THIRTEEN

"HERE YOU GO," Lyana handed Ian a fresh cup, holding hers in the other. She grabbed a blanket with her free hand, and they made their way outside.

As the two sat bundled in blankets, cupping their coffee mugs and soaking up the brisk morning air, Ian's attention turned to the lamp-post sitting at the entrance to the house. He squinted, focusing on something that looked familiar. He scoured his memory, trying to recall where he had seen the symbol before. Several minutes passed, he was still unable to place it.

He stood, intending to make his way over to inspect the symbol more closely when he glanced over and noticed Lyana was lost in one of her moments. He returned to Lyana. "Ly … Be with me," he whispered as he sat and gently held her hand.

The time she went away seemed to be growing longer with each episode, and the episodes had become more frequent since they arrived at Farr Hill.

After a minute or two, she looked up at him and offered a tired smile.

Ian desperately wanted to ask where she'd gone, what she'd seen. He wanted to understand. He wanted to help.

Instead, they enjoyed the rest of their morning routine in peaceful silence.

Later that day, after the kids had returned home from school, storm clouds rolled in and the sky began to darken. The family was gearing up for a quiet and comfortable weekend at home and in typical Friday tradition, were discussing what they would order in for dinner. The impending storm solidified their cozy weekend plans of movie watching, popcorn making, and family time.

Zach's fascination with the storm had sent him on an internet search for every piece of information about the storm he could possibly share with his family, meanwhile Ariel was sifting through takeout menus.

"I'm checking out the satellites and wind patterns and from what I can tell, the storm should be here in the next · hour," said Zach.

"What about lobster rolls or fish and chips?" asked Ariel.

The two began talking over the top of each other. It was several minutes before Ian decided to interrupt the competing monologues.

"Guys, if the weather gets too bad, I am not running out for food!" he said, peering out the window, examining the darkening sky.

They agreed on fish and chips.

Lyana called in the order while Zach joined his father at the window.

"Twenty minutes," Lyana said after hanging up. "Better go now."

As Ian began to head out, he noticed Zach's concerned expression.

"I'll be quick," Ian said. "And careful," he added. Ian patted Zach on the shoulder, then left to get the food.

By the time he started back, the rain and wind had picked up dramatically, just as Zach predicted. The wipers could barely keep up, making the winding roads difficult to see. Although they had been there a few months, Ian still wasn't that familiar with the roads, and this was his first time driving in the dark during a storm.

As the driveway neared, he sank further into his seat, gripping the wheel and leaning forward, squinting through the windshield to see more clearly.

Night here was dark, really dark—not at all like their previous neighborhood in the city lined with houses and streetlights. Out here there were no lights and the roads were crowded with tall, shadowy trees.

Ian turned onto the driveway, headlights illuminating the winding road. He knew he was nearly home when he saw the guiding light of the lamp-post. For a fleeting moment, he wondered how Marshall was faring with the storm. He realized he didn't even know where Marshall lived on the property.

As he drew closer to the house, he saw Lyana running around near the garden. He stopped before pulling into the garage and jumped out of the car to see if she needed help.

The rain was coming down in a torrent as the two of them worked together to cover the vegetable garden with row covers from the garage. After placing the final peg in the corner, they covered themselves with their rain jackets and ran to the garage. The car was still running with the headlights on.

Soaked, water running down both their cheeks, they shared a moment of laughter.

"You'd better get the car in the garage," said Lyana, water cascading from her hair. Ian was struck by how lovely she looked—like she had just stepped out of a movie. This was one of those moments he wished he could live in forever. He smiled at her, then ran back into the storm and pulled the car into the garage. Lyana grabbed the food from the passenger seat and the two made their way inside.

Ariel burst down the stairs. "I'm starving! Is the food ready?"

"Give us a minute to dry off and change clothes," said Lyana.

Lyana towel-dried herself in the kitchen and started prepping plates of food while Ian went to shower and clean up.

• • •

"Mom, it's getting really bad out there!" Zach yelled from the living room. He had been following the storm on radar and insisted it was about to get even worse. He was only able to count to three this time before the next boom of thunder.

"Let me see what's going on." Ian had returned from his shower and the two intently sat watching the news. Flash flood and severe thunderstorm warnings scrolled across the bottom of the screen.

"Lyana, it looks really rough out there. I can't think of a storm we've weathered worse than this."

Lyana looked over and offered a raised eyebrow. She almost mouthed, "Really?" but thought better of it. They had weathered worse. Metaphorically, anyway. But he knew that.

She brought the dinner plates into the living room, pausing to glance at the television between trips, then snuggled in on the couch with her food. The kids were sprawled out on the floor, eating in front of the TV. Ian was on the opposite end of the couch. All intently watched the storm reports as the wind whipped at the house, rattling the windows.

A crash of thunder so loud it shook the house startled Ariel, who let out a brief, but piercing screech. She recovered quickly and suggested they put on a movie to help pass the time. Lyana knew what she really needed was a distraction. This storm was obviously making her nervous.

As Zach called out movie choices from the DVD collection, Ian gathered empty plates and took them into the kitchen.

"*The Goonies?*"

Ian called out his "yes" to add to the chorus, then rejoined them in the living room. Everyone settled into their favorite spot for the movie night.

The storm had worsened. When lightning flashed, the entire house lit up. Lyana thought there was something both eerie and beautiful about the way the lightning brightened the room. She looked over at Ariel to see how she was faring. She was huddled into a ball. Lyana was about to say something when the brightest flash yet lit up the room. Zach barely got out a "one" before thunder followed.

And then the power went out.

Goonies never say die.

They were surrounded by darkness. The kind of darkness Lyana hadn't known since she was little, when she lived in a small town where the light pollution was minimal and moonless nights would paint her tiny world black.

Lyana rushed to the pantry to look for anything she could use to light up the house.

"I think I have a flashlight in the study," said Ian.

Lyana frantically opened and closed each drawer and cabinet. She knew she had put the matches and candles in the pantry somewhere.

Where did I put them?

She finally found them in a drawer she'd already searched through and gathered as many as she could in her hands. Lightning struck nearby again and lit up the kitchen behind her. When she looked up, she found herself face to face with the old mirror, but this time it wasn't her own face staring back at her that caught her attention. The reflection was of a child standing behind her, a little girl. Lyana was stunned into silence by what she saw. The little girl looked lost and alone. She was hugging a stuffed toy like it was her lifeline. Her pale skin stood in stark contrast to her bright red hair and dark eyes. Lyana held the matches and candles a bit tighter as the little girl behind her inched closer and reached out her hand.

"Mom, did you find them?" Ariel shouted from the living room.

Lyana dropped the candles and matches and quickly spun around. The pantry was empty. The girl was gone. With the next flash of lightning, she knelt to gather up the candles and matches. As she stood, a part of her hoped to see the little girl again, but a quick glance in the mirror revealed only a reflection of herself standing alone in the dark.

Her heart racing, she squeezed her eyes shut and took a deep breath. She struggled to shake off the unnerving vision as she returned to the living room.

FOURTEEN

I AN WAS SEARCHING for where he had put the flashlights he and Zach used on their camping trip the previous year. He knew they had packed them for the move but couldn't remember where he had placed them.

Unable to find them in his study, he used the wall to guide him as he made his way through the darkened hallway, lightly brushing his hands along the wainscotting. He stopped suddenly when his fingers grazed an unexpected ridge.

A door?

They hadn't been in the house all that long, but he was certain he had explored it thoroughly. He hadn't seen a door here before. His hands made their way to the edges, exploring to be sure it was a door. When his fingertips landed on what felt like an iron handle, he slowly twisted it, expecting to hear a squeak. Instead, it turned silently. He pushed open the door and stepped gingerly inside.

The door closed with a soft click behind him. The room was lit by a single candle. Ian walked closer to the light. He stood stunned at what was in front of him: a fully decorated Thanksgiving table with beautiful silver candelabras on either side of the centerpiece. Everything was covered in dust and cobwebs as if it had been set for many years. He reached out for the matches next to the candelabras and lit one of them. The room brightened and the dust and cobwebs instantly disappeared.

The table was just like he remembered. Thanksgiving had always been his mother's favorite holiday and she would spend days preparing. It wasn't a holiday she had celebrated as a child growing up in Ireland, so when she came to the states and experienced it for herself, she immediately fell in love with the tradition. Thanksgiving was a time to celebrate with friends and family, and she always loved a good party.

A familiar orange tablecloth, lined with ivory and gold plates, flowers and candles, decorated the table, along with the best glassware which had been purchased just for the occasion. The candles were glowing, reflecting ever so slightly off the gold on the plates.

That's when he heard her. He closed his eyes. *This isn't real. This can't be real! She's gone. I am only dreaming.* But when he opened his eyes again, everything was still the way it was all those years ago.

She was there. Humming while she prepared. The smells were exactly as he remembered. And he was there, too, as a young boy. Helping his mother.

Ian and his mother had always been close. She was always his biggest supporter. The two of them had an unbreakable bond, like many sons and mothers, but theirs went even deeper because of all they had endured together. She was his protector when he was young, and he became hers when he was older. There was a deep love and adoration between them.

Losing her was so hard and broke him in ways he never imagined. He knew the day would come, but he still wasn't prepared for it.

As he stood there staring at the scene from his childhood, he was confused.

How is this possible? What have I stumbled upon? Why am I here?

The fleeting thought was interrupted by his father appearing. An angry gust of wind preceded him, extinguishing a few candles and his mother's happy humming. The little boy tensed up. Their demeanor completely shifted with his arrival.

When he saw what his father was wearing and how he was acting, Ian knew exactly where he was.

No. I don't want to be here!

He was taken back to the very moment he had tried so hard to put out of his mind for years. He turned to leave, but the door was gone. Panic took over as his eyes surveyed the room, trying desperately to find a way out of this living nightmare.

There was nowhere for him to go. He had no choice but to face what he knew was about to happen.

His father stormed over to his mother, demanding she tell him why she had to do this every year. He despised Thanksgiving and anything that didn't revolve around him simply fueled his rage. Ian watched, powerless to help, as his father followed on her heels, harassing and taunting her with every step.

She had become immune to his tirades by then and ignored him as she continued to set the table. But then she did the unthinkable. She turned her back to him to reach for the matches so she could re-light the candles.

He snapped.

"Don't you turn your back on me!"

The words filled the room just like they had all those years ago. Ian turned to watch the young version of himself he barely recognized—innocent and unaware of what was about to happen.

"Mom, let me help you," young Ian offered, as naïve as he was excited about the holiday.

All of Ian's muscles tensed as his father lunged at his younger self, hitting him so hard he flew backwards onto the ground. The smell of alcohol hit Ian almost as hard as the slap.

His mother quickly came to his defense.

"What are you doing?" she screamed. She rushed to young Ian, who was still lying on the floor, blood dripping from his nose and the ear he had scraped on the table on the way to the ground. He was shaken by the punch, but as his vision cleared, he saw his sobbing mother in front of him. He reached out to embrace her, but before he could wrap his arms around her for comfort, his father grabbed her by her hair and lifted her from her knees, then force-fully turned her around to take his abuse head-on. As he reached around her head, old Ian tried to turn away—he knew what was coming. But it was like his own head was being held as well. He watched as his father smashed his mother's face into one of the plates, shattering it. He watched as his younger self shuddered when his father threw her to the ground.

She climbed to her knees, blood streaming down her face, and young Ian ran to her. His father stomped out of the room. They had no idea what was coming next. Ian desperately wished he could step into this scene, change the story. Make things right.

Seconds later, his father stormed back into the room and grabbed his mother by the neck, bringing her once again to her feet.

"Ian, run!" she cried out, her voice muffled by the hand around her neck.

Run, Ian, his older self echoed. He knew what the younger version of him didn't yet. His father was holding a gun to her head.

With a rush of adrenaline, young Ian lunged out to try to help his mother. His father threw her to the ground again and pointed the gun at him.

"Watch it boy or I will kill you."

Ian's mother began rising from the floor behind his father. He tried to not look at her or make any sudden moves that would tip his father off to her actions, but when the floor creaked ever so slightly, he whipped around and pointed the gun back at her.

Young Ian lay on the floor, bleeding. His mother lay bloodied across from him. His father stood between them, looking back and forth with wild eyes, unsure who to kill first.

He turned toward his mother and fired three shots.

"NO!" both Ians cried out in unison.

Young Ian ran toward her but before he could reach her, his father swung at him, hitting him on the side of the head, knocking him back to the ground.

When his father finally stumbled away, he slurred under his breath, "You think you're better than me boy? You're just like me."

I'm nothing like you older Ian wanted to scream at his drunken father, but he was frozen and unable to move. It was like a barrier stood between him and what he just watched unfold.

When young Ian came to, he went to his mother's side. Two of the three shots had hit the wall behind his mother. One had hit its intended target. She was bleeding from her stomach.

"Mom, it's going to be okay," young Ian whispered.

He ran to the phone to dial 9-1-1 and as soon as he hung up, he fell to his knees next to his mother's side, humming to her. He held her head in his lap, rocking back and forth, repeating, "Please don't leave me."

Older Ian mouthed the words along with his younger self.

The scene suddenly began to fade. The room darkened. Only the light from a single candelabra remained. Ian felt his chest tighten; he couldn't breathe. He needed to get out of there. The walls were closing in on him. He reached for the candelabra and shouted, "Let me out of here, let me out!" When his cries went unheeded, he leaned his head against the wall and said again, this time with an exhausted whisper, "Please let me out of here."

The door reappeared. He pulled it open and fell to his knees in the hallway, gasping for air. The door closed behind him without a sound.

"Dad, where have you been?" Zach practically tackled him as he tried to catch his breath.

"Zach? What are you ..."

"Dad, she's doing it again. We need help!"

Gathering himself, he lifted the candelabra to light the way and they rushed through the darkened house back to the living room where Lyana stood frozen.

"How long?"

"A few minutes," said Zach.

Ariel was crying and barely able to speak. "She just kept mumbling and staring out the window, and next thing we knew she was gone," she said between tearful gasps.

The house was still dark, but the few candles Lyana must have lit were enough for him to see her.

He reached out for her.

"Be with me, Lyana. Be with me …"

As he awaited a response, he looked out the window and noticed a bright light at the front gate.

They had been without power for hours—*how has it been hours?* Ian wondered—yet the lamp-post shined so bright, it was practically blinding.

It must have a different power source.

Ian stared, pondering how it could be. The power came back on, the lights flickered, then stayed on. Lyana blinked twice.

She was back.

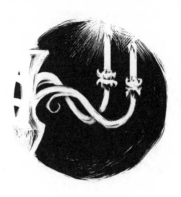

FIFTEEN

"THAT WAS WEIRD, wasn't it?" Zach said the next day as he and Ariel were outside cleaning up debris from the storm.

"I was so scared," Ariel said. "I mean, the storm was scary, but then the thing with Mom …"

Zach tossed the branches he'd collected onto the growing pile.

"I'm worried about her, Zach," she added.

"Did you write about it?" Zach knew how much she liked to spend time with her journal. It was off-limits to him, of course, but she didn't try to hide the fact that her journal was important to her. Kind of like numbers were to him.

She nodded.

"Did you see the lamp-post?" Zach asked.

Ariel brushed it off. "Yeah. But what's the big deal with that anyway? I don't get it."

"How did it stay on when *everything* else lost power? If the main line coming to the house was down, there's no way it should have been on."

"Um, news flash. I don't care." Ariel folded her arms across her chest. Zach had noticed she was doing that more often lately. "Stop talking and help with these branches so we can go back inside." She sighed, then softened her voice. "Why aren't you wearing your snake bracelet?"

"Huh?" Zach looked up from his pile of sticks. "Oh, it's a little big. It's in my display case for now."

"Where you keep all your trinkets," said Ariel, the snark back in her tone.

"They're not trinkets! They're valuables!"

Ariel shrugged. "Whatever."

As Zach gathered more branches from the back yard, he tried to organize his thoughts about last night's strange events. The lamp-post. His mother. He couldn't shake this feeling the two were connected somehow. He knew that didn't make a lot of sense, but he was curious enough to try to find the connection.

Zach liked to look at the deeper meaning of things. Where surface level information might suffice for most people, he needed details about everything—the fog, the house, his mother, the world around him. Exploring all the ways in which things were connected helped him to feel safe in a world that often didn't know exactly what to do with someone like him.

From the time he was very young, he had a way of empathizing with everyone around him—he could truly feel what others were feeling. He was the kid who would rescue wounded animals and befriend the new kid at school others were ignoring. Younger kids naturally gravitated towards him, too, sensing that he was a safe friend. Someone who wouldn't look down on them. He didn't fit in a neat box, and while he knew that brought challenges, he also knew his parents loved him just as he was.

He was seven when everything changed. Ian and Lyana had been called to school and at the request of his teacher and principal to talk about Zach's behavioral "quirks." This led to a visit with their pediatrician.

From the minute they heard *Asperger's Syndrome* his parents vowed he wouldn't live his life imprisoned by labels or expectations. Instead, they simply allowed him to be exactly who he was and embraced everything about him—the way his mind works, how he experiences the world around him. It wasn't always easy, especially in moments when his emotions would overwhelm him or when he would get frustrated because he didn't have the answer to something, but the difficult moments were always countered by a brilliant observation or beautiful sentiment about the world.

The way his family embraced him allowed Zach to thrive, but school and friendships became difficult and often left him feeling unfulfilled and lonely. Loneliness followed him through elementary and into middle school. It was in middle school that he discovered the importance of numbers. Numbers were facts that provided stability in his life, unlike people who were full of ever-changing perspectives and opinions. Counting calmed him. Gave him a sense of peace.

"Ariel, I found eight branches so far. What about you?" He went back to counting before she could even answer him. "… 9, 10, 11 …" His voice trailed off.

Ariel and Zach, although as different as two kids could possibly be, still competed over silly things like who could pick up the most branches from the yard the day after a storm. And although she found herself annoyed with her brother on most days, deep down Ariel loved his ability to remain true to who he was and the innocence that came with that.

She was three years old when he was born and from the minute he arrived, she embraced being the protective big sister. Early on, she resented not having the full attention of her parents, but the friendship she developed with her brother eventually outweighed any of that. When he was diagnosed, she noticed a shift in the dynamic and rather than embrace Zach in the same way her parents did, she started to retreat. She loved him, but deep down felt like she wasn't special. Maybe it was the way her parents treated him, or maybe it was all in her head. But that feeling of inadequacy drove her to excel in everything she did. She became the most popular girl. The star and captain of the soccer team. She got involved in everything. A quest for perfection became her outlet, but she would sit in her bedroom at night longing to have the same freedom allowed to her brother. She just wanted to be herself.

Her journals allowed her to do just that. They were her safe place.

During the three years before Zach's arrival, she was the center of her parents' world. Ariel only had vague memories of that time. Another very specific memory from that season exists for her only through the stories told by her parents: there was another Keane child the world would never know. The baby girl who was lost to a miscarriage in the years between Ariel and Zach. Ariel often thought about the little sister who she'd never meet.

"I bet I can find more than you!" she challenged with a competitive smirk.

• • •

Inside the house, Ian and Lyana stood staring at the candelabra Ian had discovered in the now missing room, comparing notes from the night before.

Ian recalled every vivid detail with trepidation. He told Lyana how he found the door and the secret room that appeared, and then went on to describe the scene that played out before his very eyes.

Lyana couldn't believe what she was hearing. She had heard the story before, of course, and knew everything about Ian's past, but to think about the possibility of a secret room taking him back to that horrific moment was just too much. She couldn't help letting her eyes wander over to the bottle on the shelf. Had it been opened?

"A secret door? Are you sure?"

He led her to the hallway and together they searched the wall for a seam or any clue that a door might exist.

"I swear it was here!" Ian said. "This candelabra proves it. Doesn't it? It was on the table in *there!*" He pointed to the blank wall.

Lyana didn't want to doubt Ian. His breath didn't smell of alcohol and she was looking at the candelabra with her own two eyes, but it was still incomprehensible, and she was still reeling from her own episode. She had no explanation for what was going on with her. She was confused and disoriented. Unlike Ian, she could barely remember what happened.

"I'm really scared Ian. It's not just about the missing secret room. I'm worried about me. What is happening to me?"

Ian wrapped his arms around her and the two stood in the hallway, her head resting on his shoulder. She felt safe in Ian's arms, but they still had no answers to the questions that surrounded the events of the last twenty-four hours.

She whispered, "Ian, I saw ..." She paused before allowing herself to say the word.

"Saw who?"

"Her."

She looked up at him with tears in her eyes. She could pinpoint the moment when he realized who she was talking about. His own eyes began to tear up.

"She was holding the stuffed lamb we got for her."

"Lyana, that's just not possible. It's not real. She's gone."

The words echoed, *it's not real.*

The line between what was real and what was not had become so blurred, Lyana was beginning to question her own sanity. *It felt real. How could it not be real?* She knew what she saw, but was she dreaming? Was she creating something in her mind that didn't exist? Was there something more happening here or was she truly losing her mind?

Ian pulled her closer and kissed the top of her head.

"It's all going to be okay, Ly. I promise, it will."

His words offered some comfort, but she heard the uncertainty in his voice.

SIXTEEN

"I THINK IT WAS right here."

Zach had convinced Ariel to go exploring, a distraction from cleaning up the rest of the yard, or maybe it was Zach's way of avoiding dealing with the fact that she had a bigger pile of sticks. Ariel was up for the adventure, though. She was tired of fetching sticks. They ventured past the back yard into the woods.

"I didn't realize how big it was!" she said as she looked around. It was the first time since they had moved that Ariel was exploring beyond the backyard. As she followed Zach, she tried to take it all in—the fog that seemed to perpetually hover at the tree line, the infinite rows of trees. It was all just so vast. It almost felt like walking into a different dimension, the real world fading behind them, just out of reach. But her sense of awe faded, replaced by a rapidly growing sense of unease. She had only known life in the city and preferred quiet moments in her room buried in her notebooks to exploring strange, spooky woods.

"Let's head back, this is creeping me out," she said.

Zach didn't stop.

"Come on! I need to show you the door in the dirt. You have to see it, Ariel. You just have to. And who knows, we might even run into Marshall."

Ariel wasn't so sure she wanted to run into Marshall, but Zach was insistent, and she didn't want to leave him out here alone. "Okay, fine, but then we need to head back."

Zach started counting the steps between trees, then paused, turned in a different direction, and repeated the action. He looked back at Ariel. "I swear it was just over here," he said, pointing.

"Okay, *now* can we head back?" said Ariel.

"Ten more minutes. I know I'll find it!"

She knew not to argue with him when he was on a mission. Lyana and Ian were patient with him in a way she was unable to be, and that awareness pushed her to keep exploring with him hoping it would soon come to an end. Looking behind her and trying to recall the path they had taken to get this far, she noticed something in the distance.

Zach was on his hands and knees, feeling the ground, insisting the door must have gotten buried by the storm. Watching him from the corner of her eye, Ariel moved toward what looked like a small clearing. The fog was dense, but just beyond the trees she could see what looked like a building.

"Zach, over here!"

Her voice echoed and Zach looked up. He stood up and ran over to her. "It's not over that way it's …" he began.

"Look, there," she interrupted. She pointed at the barely visible building.

"I said I wanted to show you the cellar door," he said, adamant. The two argued back and forth for a few minutes.

"Zach! Stop! Don't you see it? There's something over there. I know a potential secret hideout can't possibly compete with your stupid cellar door, but if I'm wrong, I'll help you look for it."

Zach sighed. "Fine. But only because you're a scaredy cat and there's no way you'd go check it out on your own."

He *was* right. She was a scaredy cat.

As they walked into the clearing, the fog thinned. Sure enough, at the back of the clearing sat a small, weather-beaten shack. Bushes and privets cloaked the shack within its natural surroundings. Ariel noted there wasn't any smoke drifting up from the crumbling brick chimney. A single window appeared on one side of building and other than that, there was nothing to alert whoever might be inside to the outside world, or that visitors were heading that way.

Ariel was not keen to continue exploring.

"This is a bad idea after all," she said. "Let's go home."

Zach continued forward, slowing his steps as they drew closer to the building.

"Hello?" Ariel called out sheepishly.

"Shh," Zach turned to her, "what if someone is in there?"

"That's kind of the point of saying 'hello'," she replied in a half-whisper. "Do you think it's smart to just show up unannounced? What if the person inside has a gun?"

Zach hesitated, but then shook his head. "I don't think anyone is here." He sneaked up to the window and carefully peered inside. "I bet this is where he lives!"

Ariel was curious but remained a safe distance behind Zach as he approached the door. Zach paused at the door, seemingly distracted by something.

"What is it?" asked Ariel.

She moved closer, trying to get a peek at what was so interesting. Zach was touching the door handle.

"It's the same. Look here." He pointed.

She had no idea what he was talking about and looked at him perplexed.

"The same as what?"

"The same as the cellar door." He pointed to a strange symbol. Ariel leaned forward to see what he was going on about, but before she got a good look, Zach opened the door. She stopped dead in her tracks.

"What are you doing?" She did not want anything to do with this obvious invasion of privacy. "You can't go inside. That's trespassing!" she said. *What if someone lived there? What if it was dangerous?*

Zach went in anyway.

He stood in the entryway. Ariel looked over his shoulder, taking in what looked like someone's living quarters. It smelled damp with a slight hint of soot. There was a small wood stove in the corner, complete with a kettle and saucepan, a single mattress elevated ever so slightly, a small table with unfinished carving projects, and a pair of what appeared to be beekeeper's gloves. The window was covered with a sheet of cloth so thin it barely kept out any light. A window covering that translucent meant that whoever lived here could clearly see if anyone was coming. Dust hung in the air and covered bookshelves that lined the entire shack.

"What is all this stuff?" Zach took a few steps inside the shack, then reached over to touch the nearest shelf. "Dad would love this!"

"Enough, Zach, let's go!"

But he didn't budge. Once he got an idea in his head …

Zach was staring at the table at an open notebook with what looked like strange symbols scribbled on the pages. As Ariel looked around, she noticed hundreds of old books filled the dusty shelves, along with strange artifacts. There was a picture hanging on the wall that resembled an ancient symbol. Then she saw something that made her heart skip a beat.

"Zach, is that your …" She pointed to a shelf.

"My what?" Zach turned to look where she was pointing. Looped over a wing of a carved wooden eagle was a bracelet. A bracelet that looked just like Zach's. "It can't be," he said, walking toward it. Mine is …"

Ariel shuddered. This was wrong. Creepy and wrong. She shuffled backward out of the doorway and tripped. The sound of her falling startled Zach, who quickly turned his attention toward his sister. She was about to ask him to help her up, but he was looking past her, toward the forest. Then she heard it, too. A shuffling sound.

"Zach … it's time to go. Now!"

Zach quickly shut the door behind him and ran to his sister. The rustling was getting louder. Whoever, or whatever was coming was approaching fast. He reached out for her hand and helped her to her feet. The two of them ran headlong into the fog and back into the woods, not looking behind them even once. They just ran, quickly and as silently as the forest floor would allow. As they ran deeper into the woods, the fog thickened again, and the trees began to close in.

"Which way do we go?" yelled Ariel.

"I don't know! I can't find the path!"

Zach was a natural navigator, but if *he* couldn't tell if they were running in the right direction, they were in big trouble.

"I hope we're heading the right way," Ariel said. They were about to give up, when suddenly they emerged from the woods and into the back yard, breathless, leaning over, winded from the run.

"Don't tell Mom and Dad, okay?" said Zach. "They would be furious." Even though Zach was a young man, they were still protective parents, especially since everyone was still getting used to life outside the city. The woods represented the unknown. And the unknown was scary for parents.

Ariel raced to the house, and Zach quickly followed behind. He knew she was going to tell them everything.

The two entered the house in a rush of noise, talking over one another as each explained their version of what happened to their parents.

"One at a time," Lyana said. "One at a time."

"Ariel first," said Ian.

Zach let out a defeated sigh as Ian pointed to her to go first. As Ariel recounted the events from the last several hours, she watched her parents' eyes turn to Zach, staring at him in disapproval.

He tried to interrupt and was shut down each time.

"Is all of this true?" Ian asked.

"Well …"

Ariel interrupted him. "You already know it's true!"

Of course they did. It wasn't the first time Zach's curiosity had gotten the better of him and it wouldn't be the last.

Frustrated, Zach started yelling at Ariel and the two began fighting again. Their escalating anger consumed the room like a black cloud hanging over them.

"That's enough now!" shouted Ian. He so rarely raised his voice, Ariel stopped speaking immediately. Zach soon followed suit. Ian told the kids to go upstairs and get cleaned up for dinner. "We'll talk about this later," he added as they sulked away.

The two of them made their way up the stairs. Zach gave Ariel a dirty look.

Ariel paused in the hallway to watch him walk over to his display case. His bracelet was still there. *Just a strange coincidence*, she thought. Then she continued into her own room. She ran over to the intercom system, pressed the button for Zach's room and exclaimed, "You couldn't just leave it alone." The fact that he got in trouble gave her so much satisfaction.

Zach's voice came back over the intercom, "Shut up!"

She pressed the button to offer a retort, or maybe an apology, but he had muted her channel.

And with that, the conversation was over.

• • •

Zach was still upset and pacing around his room, trying to ease his frustration. He wrapped himself in his blanket like a burrito, a trick that usually worked when he was overwhelmed. As the grasp of big emotions began to diminish, he whispered under his breath.

"Why does she always have to be right?!"

By the time dinner was ready, Zach had calmed himself and moved on from the fight with his sister. He joined his parents downstairs. As they waited for Ariel, the three of them talked about the kids' adventure, with his parents reiterating the importance of communicating where they are, and if they go into the woods, to make sure an adult knows or goes with them.

"It's just, we don't know what to expect out here …" said Ian.

Ian was interrupted by the sound of stomping feet coming down the stairs. When Ariel approached, she was hysterical. She raced round in circles, arms flailing in the air, pointing at her throat.

"Slow down! What is it?" Lyana asked with obvious concern in her voice. "Use your words!"

And just as her mother uttered the words, Ariel stopped. She started opening and closing drawers, finally grabbing a pad of paper and a pencil. Zach looked over at the note she had written.

I can't. My voice is gone!

"Oh honey, I am so sorry," said Lyana, putting her arm around Ariel.

"It must have been that cold air in the forest," offered Ian.

Zach wasn't so sure that was the case, remembering the words he shouted at her just before he muted her on the intercom.

Something didn't feel right. Panic started to rise in his own throat. But his parents didn't seem to think it was anything more than strained vocal cords. His mom would know a thing or two about that from all her musical training. And maybe she was right.

But as Zach grabbed a glass of water and quietly made his way to the stairwell, his thoughts were spinning. *Is this all my fault? Did I put a curse on my sister?*

Zach counted the steps on his way upstairs.

"… 13, 14, 15."

SEVENTEEN

ZACH HAD TOSSED and turned for hours, worried he might have been the one who silenced his sister. He didn't fully understand how, but it was just too coincidental to ignore. His mom had always warned him to be careful with his words when he was angry or upset, and the guilt was eating at him. Had he done this?

He finally fell asleep, only to be awakened what seemed like minutes later by an intense and confusing dream. He sat up in a panic, breathing heavily and sweating. It was early in the morning, hours before sunrise. He lay back down and tried to control his breathing while attempting to recall the details of his dream. His thoughts were interrupted as he remembered Ariel. He tentatively got out of bed and walked over to the intercom. He whispered under his breath, "I didn't mean it," and unmuted his sister's channel, then crawled back in bed.

Maybe this will fix things.

A few hours later he came down the stairs feeling exhausted and anxious.

Much to his surprise and relief, Ariel was in the kitchen talking with Lyana over breakfast. The two were chatting like nothing happened. He couldn't believe it.

It worked! But how?!

He stood just outside of the kitchen, listening, absently spinning the bracelet on his wrist. But it wasn't the sound of Ariel's voice that surprised him most. It was her words. She was sharing the details from a dream she had the night before.

"Mom, it was the strangest dream! I was a little boy," Ariel began. "Some of the details are fuzzy, you know? But other parts? I can still picture them, like they were from a movie."

Zach knew exactly what that was like; some memories of a dream are vivid, others are like a broken windowpane—difficult to piece together. She continued her recollection.

"It was like an ancient time in a foreign land. I can't quite place the time period, but I've seen something similar in Dad's history books. As I said, I was a little boy, a slave held captive by soldiers and older men with long beards who wore colorful robes and strange hats." She paused. "You know how you're like the main character and also looking in on the main character in dreams? It was like that. I could sense the boy's—my—apprehension, looking over at the commotion near a large tent that had been set up near a stone archway and what appeared to be a temple of some sort."

Lyana pushed the brew button on the coffee pot. "Go on."

"One of the men in robes commanded a soldier to go inside the temple, but before he went, they tied a rope to his ankle. A few moments after he disappeared, I heard screams from inside the tent … where I think soldiers were stationed? Maybe not. Anyway, a team of soldiers grabbed the rope and pulled his body out of the temple. I'm pretty sure he was dead. They repeated this many times. I don't know how many—numbers are weird in dreams sometimes—but the robed men were growing impatient and more frustrated with each failed attempt. Their leader, a tall man with a big, weird hat and intricately decorated robe, called to the soldiers and pointed at the young boy. At *me*. His ... my heart raced as they grabbed the rope and tied it to my ankle. I knew what was coming next ..."

The conversation lulled as Zach entered the kitchen. Lyana got up to grab her coffee.

"Ariel, I need to check on something, but I really do want to hear the rest of your dream. Can it wait until later?"

Ariel sighed, then nodded. "Yeah, it can wait."

Once the two of them were alone, Zach couldn't help himself. "What was that story you were telling Mom?"

"I had this crazy dream last night." Ariel was shaking her head.

Zach was relieved she was speaking again and wanted to hear more.

"How much have you heard," she asked.

"I think I caught it all. The little boy had a rope tied to his leg ..."

"Right. So, the soldiers tied the rope around the boy's ankle. He was so young, yet they all looked to him with hope. I think he was their last hope. Once the rope was secured, they pushed him to his knees and motioned for him to crawl through the entrance to the tent. He did as he was told. This is where it gets fuzzy a bit, because I'm sort of the boy and I'm not, you know? But I remember crawling on all fours, pressed close to the floor and entering a darkened and vast space. The soldiers just outside the entrance pulled on the rope, then, calling out to him. He pulled back on the rope twice to signal he was okay. He then turned and kept moving forward."

"This is crazy!" Zach interrupted.

Ariel quickly responded, "I know, it was so weird and felt so real!"

"No, you don't understand," Zach couldn't believe what he was hearing. "I had a dream too!"

"So what?"

"I had the *same* dream!"

The two paused and exchanged a look of shock and confusion. They began excitedly comparing details from each other's dream.

In Zach's dream, he was also a young boy, but he was standing outside the entrance to the temple, watching as soldiers knelt to place a rope around another boy's ankle. He couldn't tell if he knew the boy or was just a bystander. He was scared for the boy, who was around his age, maybe a little younger. He wanted to help but was frozen and unable to move.

"How is this possible?" Ariel asked. "This makes no sense. There's no way you could have been in my dream, watching it play out. That's ... crazy."

"What happened next?" Zach asked. He was almost breathless with anticipation.

Ariel was animated and acting out as she described inching closer and closer to something, crawling along the sandy floor. She remembered a strange feeling, a surprising sense of comfort, like he wasn't scared. This place was *familiar* to him. All those soldiers had come and gone, losing their lives in the process, yet this young slave boy instinctively knew what to do.

"It was like he had been there before," she said. "Like *I* had been there before."

Zach was hanging on to her every word. "Then what happened?"

His dream had ended as they sent the boy into the temple. The image haunted him. In his dream, he had watched as the soldiers lost their lives, one by one. He was so afraid when they placed the rope on the young boy, the men not caring if he lost his life. The thought of the boy not coming back out alive was too much for Zach to bear. The image that was seared into his brain from the dream was that of the young boy looking at him and nodding directly at him with a sheepish smile before crawling into the temple.

"This is so insane! I looked at a boy before crawling inside!" Ariel was as animated as Zach had ever seen her. He felt a similar energy as he stood there listening, waiting, hoping she knew what came next.

"What happened inside the temple?" Zach could hardly contain himself.

"It was the strangest thing. And … I mean I'll tell it from the way I saw it. But keep in mind, I'm this boy."

"Got it."

"Once inside this huge room, out of sight or sound of the men and soldiers, I pushed myself up from the floor and onto my feet. It was so dark. I turned and looked toward the entrance behind me to make sure I couldn't be seen, then reached into my pocket. I was holding something. As I slowly opened my hand, I saw that a stone shone so brightly, it lit up the entire room. It sparkled with every color of the rainbow, but the red flickered like fire. It was mesmerizing! I knew in that moment that I was—and I know how this sounds, Zach, but listen—I knew that I was in the presence of this most powerful God, the God of *my* people. This boy's people, anyway. I placed the stone at the foot of the altar, and it continued to glow. It was like the stone was channeling the strength in the temple. Then I looked around and grabbed the stone, placing it safely back inside my pocket."

"What do you think it means? What happened next?" Zach had so many questions. He desperately wanted more of the story.

"I tugged on the rope," she said. Ariel reached for the orange juice and poured herself another glass.

"Then what?"

"I woke up," she said nonchalantly and sipped her juice.

"That's it? You just woke up?"

Ariel insisted that is where it ended, then just shrugged.

Zach grabbed a bowl and some cereal, his mind still racing from the conversation. The lamp-post, Lyana's episode, the cellar door, the intercom, and now the dream. There were just too many things happening all at once for it to be a coincidence. He couldn't shake this feeling that it was somehow all connected. He desperately wanted to find the missing link.

What is going on here?

He sat staring at the bowl in front of him, not breaking concentration.

"What's up with you?" Ariel was confused as Zach seemed distant and distracted.

He brushed her off and quickly finished his cereal, not offering a response. He knew if anyone could help him make sense of things, his dad could. The two of them could sit for hours reading about the historical significance of something or talk about random things like weather patterns and aliens.

He rinsed his bowl and placed it in the dishwasher before heading to the study to talk with his dad.

As he approached, he could hear his parents talking. He couldn't quite make out what they were saying, so he leaned closer, putting his ear up to the door. He was able to catch a few words here and there.

"Ian, it's not there."

"I can't make sense of it either, but I swear it was there."

"Are you sure you didn't imagine it?"

"I know what I saw! I have the candelabra to prove it!"

Zach was surprised by the intensity in his father's voice. Hearing footsteps nearing, he quickly backed away. Ian stepped out of the study and into the hallway.

"Oh hey, Dad." Zach played it off like he had just arrived and had no idea his parents were deep in conversation behind the study door. He could also sense his dad's frustration, so he decided not to ask him to help solve the puzzle that was insistently tugging at his brain.

"You okay?" his dad asked.

"Yeah, I'm fine. I'm just going to do some research … on something. I'll be up in my room."

"Have fun, kiddo."

Ian turned and went down the hall just as Lyana emerged from the study. She seemed distracted. She barely acknowledged him.

Zach walked up the stairs, counting each one, always ending at fifteen, then sat at his desk in his room. He pulled a notebook out of the drawer and went about trying to recreate the symbol he had seen at Marshall's shack. His first attempt was nowhere close. He crumpled the paper and tossed it on the floor, then started again. His second attempt wasn't any better. Fifteen minutes later, the floor was littered with crumpled paper, and he still hadn't gotten it right. Maybe he was just remembering it wrong?

Staring at the pile of crumpled paper, he got up and made his way to Ariel's room. He poked his head inside and before he spoke a single word, she shot him a look of disgust.

"Get out of my room!" she shouted.

"Wait. I have a question."

She sighed the biggest sigh Zach had ever seen. Obviously, it was a demonstration for him of her frustration. "Fine, what?"

"Do you remember the shack?"

"What kind of a question is that? Of course I do."

"I mean, did you look at the door? The handle? Do you remember me telling you to look at it?

Ariel gave him a confused expression. "Yeah, I remember you telling me to look at it—but then you broke into the shack and that kinda distracted me."

"I didn't break in. The door was unlocked," Zach insisted.

"We weren't supposed to be there, Zach. That's someone else's property."

"Yeah, Marshall's."

"We don't know that for sure," said Ariel.

He was sure of it. "And then, what, you thought he'd stolen my bracelet?"

"It looked similar, okay? I was …"

"Go ahead and say it," said Zach.

"Fine. I was wrong." She looked down at his wrist. "You figured out how to make it smaller."

He nodded. Ariel's disgust had softened into an expression Zach had seen more than a few times before. She was dialing it down so as not to upset him. But he wasn't upset, he was frustrated.

He turned and left, heading downstairs to see if he could find anything that might spark a connection with the incomplete picture that floated in his head. After a few more failed attempts at drawing, he decided to go exploring instead. He was certain he had seen the symbol somewhere else, and surely if he went looking, he would find it.

He was intently scanning every corner of the house, moving from room to room, lost in his own world with no concept of anyone around him. Opening doors and drawers. Looking up and down, side to side.

And still nothing. His search left him empty handed and back at square one. He usually was so good at remembering things. Why was he struggling to remember this symbol?

He stood in the living room feeling defeated and noticed his mother outside, sitting quietly.

"That's it! Maybe there's a clue outside!"

He was single-minded as he walked out the front door to continue his search for clues, ignoring anything and anyone around him. He was so focused, he almost didn't hear his mother call out to him.

"Zach," she called out. "Come over here."

He turned toward her. It took a second for his brain to register what she had asked. He put his search on pause and made his way over to his mother. She reached out her hand as he approached. "Sit with me," she said.

The two sat quietly for a moment. Zach wondered what his mother wanted, but he decided that maybe she just wanted to sit with him for a bit. He bit his lip for as long as he could, but then he couldn't help himself. The biggest thing pressing on his mind, apart from the symbol he couldn't quite recreate, was his mother's "episodes".

"Mom …" He hesitated. "Are you okay?"

It was a loaded question.

"I'm …" She paused and took a deep breath. Then she began to tell him about all the ways she'd been feeling since they moved to Farr Hill. She talked about the moments of forgetting, of not knowing what was real, of the near-constant fog in her brain.

"Like the woods!" Zach interrupted. Zach sensed her worry and felt it deeply himself.

"Yes, that's … yes, that's exactly what it's like," she said, "foggy." She offered him a reassuring smile. "But you know, I'm sure everything is going to be fine. I think maybe it's just taking me some time to adjust to …" She paused and spread her arms out, indicating the whole of their expansive property. "… everything."

At that word, her arms still spread out, she seemed to freeze in place, her eyes glazing over. Zach knew that look.

"Mom, it's okay," said Zach. He waited to see if she heard him. Her arms dropped to her side, and she looked him in the eye. Zach breathed a sigh of relief. She was back to normal. "I think I understand," he added. "I've noticed several strange things too since we moved in."

"Like what?" his mother asked. She was fully attentive to him now.

"Like, this whole thing. I mean, things have been strange since we moved, right? I don't mean like unfamiliar—that's kinda the way things are at a new place. I mean, it just feels like everything is connected somehow. I don't mean just your episodes, but the door in the dirt and the shack and the symbol and Marshall and …" He paused, something important was lurking at the edge of his thoughts, like a mirage you can't see if you look at it head-on.

"Is everything okay, Zach?" his mother asked. She placed her hand on his arm.

The lamp-post!

"The storm knocked out all the lights, right?" he said, excitement growing in his voice. His mother nodded. "But not the lamp-post. The lamp-post light was still on." *That's it,* he thought. *That's got to be the missing piece.*

"Thanks, Mom. You've helped a bunch, but I gotta check something out." He jumped up and made his way toward the lamp-post. He felt his excitement, and his certainty grow with every step. But before he reached it, he heard his father call out.

"Zach!"

He turned. His mother had moved from the patio chair to the garden but there was no sign of his father. He turned back toward the lamp-post when he faintly heard it again.

"Zach, come here!"

He turned once again toward the house; he still couldn't see his dad. Thinking he must be around the back, he jogged to the opposite side of the house but found nothing. He looked around, confused.

"Dad, where are you?" he called out. All he heard in return was the sound of the rustling leaves on the ground.

"Dad? I can't find you!" Out of nowhere, the wind picked up in intensity. The trees bent and swayed, like peasants bowing before an invisible king. Zach shivered. The lamp-post would have to wait—he needed to go back into the house. He was about to tell his mother to go inside, too, but when he turned to look for her, she was gone.

EIGHTEEN

A S ZACH MOVED around the house looking for his dad, something felt off. It was like the house was moving with him, the walls shifting, the floors turning this way and that. His movements were matched with each corner he turned, like a dance. The two were moving in unison but one was leading the other. As Zach continued, he found himself walking down a long, narrow hallway. This wasn't a hallway he'd ever seen before. The ceiling was too low and with only one small window at the very end, there was just a sliver of light to guide him.

"Dad?" he cautiously called out as he wandered around another unfamiliar corner studying his surroundings. Nothing looked right. And then he saw it: the symbol! It was on a door handle that he'd never seen before.

This shouldn't be here, he thought. *None of this should be here.*

Tentatively, he reached out to touch the handle.

"Zach, what are you doing?"

He turned around to see his dad standing there in the unfamiliar hallway.

"Check this out Dad, it's the same …" Zach turned to show his father what he had found, but as he pointed to the place where the door handle was, it was gone. He was pointing at a blank wall.

"The same? As what?" his dad asked.

Frustration and confusion consumed Zach. "It was right there! I saw it." He punched at the blank wall. "Ugh! Never mind."

The hallway had returned to normal. There was no secret door. No handle with the strange symbol. Zach ran past his father up to his room.

He began drawing again, frantically this time—scouring his fuzzy brain to find the symbol. But it continued to evade him. He added a half dozen more crumpled papers to the floor, then gave up and started pacing across his room, kicking the paper absently, whispering under his breath. *Why can't I remember? What's happening to my brain?*

He dropped onto his bed and buried his face in his pillow. Just as suddenly, he flipped over and stared up at the wall. He needed to count something, but there was nothing to count there; the wall was blank.

And then, it wasn't.

Zach closed, then opened his eyes again to be sure it was real. It was. The symbol was right there on the wall—faint, but visible.

What? He couldn't believe he hadn't noticed it before. *Had it been there the entire time?* The image was subtle, almost like a watermark, but it was there, like someone had etched it onto the wall and then painted over it.

He quickly grabbed his notebook and ripped a single piece of paper from it, placing it on the wall. He took his pencil and began scribbling, watching as the outline of the symbol appeared on the paper. His eyes grew large and he smiled with pride. It was everything he had been trying to recreate.

He took the drawing and sat down at his desk, pulling open his laptop to start researching its origin. He clicked from picture to picture, article to article in search of something similar. The first search turned up nothing, so he typed in new search criteria and hit Enter. As he did, he heard a strange sound coming from the other side of his room.

"What is *that?*" he whispered to himself.

It was coming from the wall. He got up to inspect the sound and stood just inches from the wall, straining to hear the odd sound. It was a low hum or a buzzing noise. He reached out to touch the wall. As he did, the wall peeled away and turned to ash, crumbling to the floor. What he saw there froze him in disbelief.

Behind the wall was a fully viable beehive. Honeycomb filled the space between the boards that framed the wall.

Before he could process what he had found, the bees attacked. Zach covered his ears. The sound of hundreds of bees overwhelmed him. In seconds, Zach was engulfed by the swarm, being stung left and right. As excruciating pain consumed his body, he somehow managed to scream for help.

Ariel was the first to arrive at Zach's room. She saw what was happening and ran back for help, shutting the door behind her.

"Dad!" she screamed from the top of the steps. "Help!"

• • •

Ian heard the scream through the fog of a single swallow of whiskey, then stumbled out of the office. He cleared his head, steadied himself and took the stairs two at a time to discover a hysterical Ariel standing outside Zach's closed door.

"Bees! There are bees in Zach's room and they're attacking him!" she shouted.

Lyana joined Ian outside Zach's room mere seconds later. She had been in the kitchen, rinsing vegetables from the garden.

Without waiting for an explanation, she threw the door open to Zach's room. Ian was shocked when he looked inside and saw the number of bees surrounding Zach. He was engulfed in a cloud of yellow and black. It didn't look real. *Am I hallucinating?* he wondered.

Lyana screamed, then ran over to the window. She threw it open and shouted, "Khoosh! Khoosh t'looq!"

Immediately, the bees gathered and flew outside as one.

Ian was as dumbfounded by Lyana's actions as he was scared for Zach.

He had heard words like that only once before, in a graduate school class on ancient languages. *How did she know that word?*

Lyana raced to Zach, who was lying on the ground, motionless. She dropped to her knees.

"Call 9-1-1!" she screamed. "Now!"

Ian was already dialing. It took him two tries to get it right. He swore to himself this was the last time he would ever drink again. *Who messes up dialing 9-1-1?* He stayed on the line with the dispatcher as he knelt next to Lyana. Zach's breathing was labored. Welts were rising up on his face and neck.

Lyana sunk her face onto her son's chest, crying uncontrollably. She sat up and placed his head on her lap. "Please don't leave. I can't lose you, too …"

"They're on their way," said Ian. "Hold on, son. Hold on." He placed his hand gently against his son's swelling cheek.

Please hold on.

NINETEEN

"**D**ID YOU HEAR what happened out at Farr Hill?"

The café was stirring as word traveled quickly through the town that the youngest member of the Keane family was taken to the hospital by ambulance the night before. The whispers ebbed and flowed, punctuated by nervous glances and theories, some believable, some wild.

Lloyd was making the rounds, filling cups and greeting patrons who were mumbling about what had occurred.

"I heard," he responded hesitantly.

He had come to know the Keane family well; they were weekend regulars at the café. Saturday morning pancake breakfasts had become their staple, and he got to know Zach in particular because he always had something interesting to say. Their conversations were a weekend highlight for Lloyd. Zach reminded him of his own son who was now grown up and living in New York City.

They had only missed a few weekends since their arrival in Littleton, but their absence this weekend felt heavy as Zach's fate hung in the balance.

As soon as he had heard the news, Lloyd had decided he would prepare meals to take to the family. He planned on closing the café early so he could drop one off later that day. In all his years, he could count the times he closed up shop early on one hand. One of those times felt all too familiar— the day his wife and daughter had been in a car accident. His wife walked away with just a few scrapes and bruises, but his daughter wasn't so lucky. The two were driving to Vermont to visit her family when they were struck by another car that had run a stoplight. His daughter was airlifted to Dartmouth—Hitchcock, where she remained in the ICU for several weeks. She survived the accident, but was never the same since. She had been paralyzed from the waist down.

The situation with Zach brought so many emotions to the surface of what he had walked through with his daughter. Lloyd would do anything to help.

TWENTY

"**H**E'S A REALLY lucky kid."

By the time the ambulance arrived at the hospital, Zach was in anaphylactic shock and the medical team had to work swiftly to reduce the swelling in his airway so they could intubate him. Once they were able to get his breathing regulated, they examined the extent of the injuries and were shocked at what they saw.

Doctors estimated he had been stung between 300 and 400 times. His whole body was swollen and even after they were certain his breathing was under control, they warned that the pain would be agonizing, and they needed to do all they could to keep the swelling down. It was touch and go through the long night and once his vitals were stable, he was put in a medically induced coma.

Zach was hardly recognizable lying in the hospital bed, wrapped with bandages, hooked up to a tangle of tubes and noisy machines. Nurses came and went as the minutes turned into hours.

The morning sun was finally shining through the window, painting Zach's face ever so slightly in amber.

Lyana and Ian had met so many different members of the hospital staff in the past few hours, all of whom worked tirelessly to save their son. Lyana just couldn't bring herself to leave his side. She felt the warmth of the sun hitting her back, one eye on Zach and the other watching intently as Ian discussed their son with the doctor just outside the door to his hospital room.

"He's not in the clear just yet," said Dr. Rapha. He looked in at her then, as if realizing he had spoken too loudly.

Lyana watched as Dr. Rapha grabbed Ian gently by the arm and led him away from the door. The two glanced back at her and kept talking. They were too far away for her to make out what they were saying, and she was too tired to give much thought to it.

"Coffee for you." Ariel approached Ian and handed him a cup of coffee from the cafeteria. "It's the best I could do." She shrugged, clearly trying to force even the smallest of smiles. She walked into the room and offered the other cup to her mother.

"Let's talk more about that later," Lyana heard the doctor say.

Dr. Rapha turned and went down the hallway and Ian returned to the room, sipping his coffee.

"What did he say?" Ariel asked. Lyana could tell Ariel was putting on a brave face, but knew she was feeling shattered and worried about her brother.

"The next few days will be important," he answered. He lifted the coffee cup. "Thanks for the coffee, Ariel. It was a thoughtful gesture."

"What *else* did he say?" asked Lyana.

Ian explained that the doctors needed to remove all the stingers and any bees that he may have swallowed to ensure venom didn't continue to attack his system.

"Isn't that what they were doing all night?" asked Ariel.

"They got most of them, but they have to be sure. They're also paying close attention to his brain. The goal is to keep his brain from swelling and allow his body to work at healing while he sleeps. The medicines will help with that, too."

Lyana flinched at the mention of possible brain swelling, then quickly regained what composure she could manage. She needed to be strong for Ariel.

"How long ..." Ariel began. She couldn't finish the question.

"It could be days," Ian began, "or weeks. We're going to have to be patient and trust the process here. I know that's not easy, but ... we can do this. Zach can do this. He's strong."

Ian leaned over and placed his hand gently on Zach's heavily-bandaged hand. "You can do this, buddy. I know you can."

His voice cracked and Lyana couldn't hold back the tears anymore. Ian looked over at her, but it was Ariel who came to her first, wrapping her arms around her mother.

"Dad's right. Zach can do this. He can do anything," she said. Then she added with a half-smile, "the little jerk."

That brought a tiny laugh from Lyana, and a faux glare from Ian. But then he smiled, too.

Lyana took a moment to study the room. She'd been there for hours but had spent all that time focused on Zach. There were at least a dozen bouquets of flowers stationed around the room—on the windowsill, the small desk area, and even by the sink near the door. She got up and went from bouquet to bouquet, reading the attached notes.

Thinking of you. Lloyd and the café crew.

Don't forget, you're not alone. Kelly Garner.

Ian stood suddenly, as if he'd just gotten an idea.

"What is it, Ian?" asked Lyana.

"Since we don't know how long we're going to be here, I'm going to run back to the house and collect some things."

"Are you sure you want to go? Now?"

"Zach is stable and there isn't much for me to do here." He paused. "I almost forgot, I talked to Lloyd down at the café and he's going to bring some food over for us a little later. I'll be back by then."

"I'll come with," said Ariel. "I want to get a few things myself. Like some clothes and my journal."

"Of course," said Ian.

Lyana couldn't bear the thought of leaving. She made a list of items for Ian and Ariel to pack and sent them on their way.

"Don't be too long," she said, and they walked quietly out of the room.

"We're here for you, Zach," Lyana whispered after they left. "And we'll wait as long as we have to."

But don't be too long.

TWENTY-ONE

W HEN THE TWO of them arrived back at the house, it was eerily silent. Vegetables that had been abandoned remained on the countertop, drawers were open from searching for the keys. It all looked the same minus a few remnants from the commotion of the night before, but it wasn't the same. Not at all. Ian stood at the bottom of the steps still processing how close they'd come to losing Zach.

"Dad, come look at this."

Ariel had rushed up to her room to start packing and was standing outside Zach's room. Ian practically ran up the stairs to join her, fearing that it was happening all over again.

They stood in the doorway to Zach's room staring. Ian gently placed his arm around Ariel. Together they silently soaked in the magnitude of what had happened the night before.

"Dad, how? Where did the bees come from?"

"I don't know. It doesn't make any sense."

The hole in the wall remained. The carpet was littered with plaster and dust. Just beyond the hole was the now empty space that was once home to the hive. While the medics worked on Zach, the firefighters cleared out the hive to make sure the bees wouldn't return.

Would they return? Ian wondered. He shivered involuntarily.

"Ariel, you pack. I'm going to go find Marshall."

On the drive home, Ian had told her that he planned to find Marshall to see if he could help them understand what was going on. He wanted to understand why so many families had come and gone from Farr Hill. There were too many strange things happening to his family, too many disparate pieces of a puzzle he couldn't piece together. And he didn't like the story those pieces were telling. Marshall must have some answers.

Ian pressed her to remember exactly where she and Zach had gone when they discovered the shack. He asked her to make a map of whatever she could remember. She worked on that while he gathered travel bags from the large closet in the hallway.

"Here you go." She handed him a crude map. "It's the best I can do. The details are a bit foggy." She laughed an awkward laugh. "Foggy, like the woods."

Ian gave her a hug. "I'm sure this will help."

She handed him the map and went back to packing. As he went down the stairs, he heard her call out, "Be careful, Dad!"

Studying the map in his hands, he didn't look up as he stepped into the back yard. When he finally felt like he had a sense of which way to go, he looked up and noticed smoke hovering over the fire pit. He went over to investigate the smoke. *This must have been how they destroyed the hive,* he thought to himself. *But why would firefighters leave a fire pit burning?*

As he stood there looking at the pit, he asked himself for the hundredth time, *How did a beehive get in the wall?* It made absolutely no sense. Very little over the last several days made sense.

"How are you holding up?"

Startled, Ian dropped the map. He turned around to see Marshall standing behind him, an ash-darkened shovel in his hands.

Ian bent down to pick up the map and slid it into his back pocket.

"Marshall," he said. "I was just going to go looking for you."

"And here I am." He dug into the dirt outside of the firepit and scooped up a shovelful, then dumped it on the smoking embers. "Firefighters ought to know better," he said. "Those embers were still hot this morning."

The two of them stood staring at the fire-pit.

"Zach going to be okay?" Marshall broke the silence, startling Ian again.

Ian was surprised Marshall remembered Zach's name. They'd only met the one time in the woods. "Thankfully, yes. The doctors are very encouraging," said Ian. "Look, Marshall, I have a few questions I need to ask you about the house."

"About the bees," said Marshall. It wasn't a question. "This isn't my first encounter with bees," he said, talking as if he had been the one to find them in the wall, not Zach. "Many years ago …" he paused. "Over the years, I've learned a thing or two about bees. Far more than I might have imagined …" He seemed lost in thought, then suddenly snapped back to the moment. "Wasps, too. Nasty things, wasps. Bees are mostly good, but … well, as you know they can do plenty of harm in a swarm when agitated."

Marshall looked down into the firepit and paused again. Then he shook his head, *perhaps to clear the cobwebs*, thought Ian. He continued, "I got here a little after the firefighters. You folks had already been whisked away in the ambulance."

The wind turned suddenly and blew the thinning smoke into Ian's face. He coughed, then cleared his throat. He needed answers.

"Marshall, you know this property. You've seen people come and go. Surely you can answer my questions."

Marshall nodded. "Perhaps I can."

"There's so much here that doesn't make sense. I don't know how to say it without sounding crazy, but … what is going on with this house?"

"That's a rather broad question, Ian."

"Surely, you've seen things that don't make sense. It's … it's hard to explain." Ian paused. When Marshall didn't respond, he continued. "Why did all the previous families leave? Did they … see things, too? Is that why they left? We've heard some of the rumors in town …" Ian shook his head, frustrated with his inability to clearly explain all that had transpired in the house, and unsure just how much detail to reveal. "Help me understand," he said. His voice held more than a tinge of desperation. He took another deep breath, this time a smoke-free one.

"Rumors," said Marshall.

"What?"

"You heard rumors, and that's all that they were. People came and went over the years. They all had good reasons to leave. One family left for a new job. Another to be closer to family. You can't rely on rumors, Ian."

"But …" Ian began. Marshall interrupted him.

"I can't tell you exactly why it didn't work out for those families. Maybe this house just wasn't for them. It's been my experience that the right home can provide the right things to the right family just when they need it."

Ian thought that was a curious answer. Was he suggesting that this house wasn't for them? Or that it explicitly was? And if it was, what could a beehive that nearly killed his son possibly have to do with that? He wasn't going to tell Marshall about *everything*. He didn't know if he could trust him. There was something about him that still felt off. Zach had called their earlier encounter "weird." Zach was right on the money.

Zach.

His phone rang. He fumbled for it, then clicked to receive the call.

"This is Ian."

TWENTY-TWO

ARIEL HAD FINISHED packing and was bringing bags downstairs, one by one, so they were ready for her dad to put them in the car. Just as she placed the final bag by the door leading to the garage, she realized she forgot to pack her journal.

"I'm an idiot," she said to herself, shaking her head in disbelief. It was the one thing she *wanted* to bring and couldn't believe that in the rush of trying to pack she nearly forgot. She had been distracted by answering texts from people inquiring about what had happened or offering comfort. It wasn't the number of people who reached out that surprised her—including more than a few new friends from school—it was that they actually seemed to care. She had spent so much time trying to be part of the popular crowd and being the perfect student and star athlete that she wasn't well acquainted with real friendship. Before moving here, her friendships with peers had always felt so superficial, and chasing their acceptance had left her feeling empty and lonely. She was desperate to connect with people who would see her for who she truly was and accept her anyway, warts and all. While she was good at playing the extrovert, the go-getter, she was really an introvert who would prefer a corner couch and a good book to parties or winning the big game.

Her journal was sitting on the white vanity table among a haphazard collection of makeup and brushes. She had an old coffee mug filled with pens and pencils on the table, too. She grabbed the journal and a few pens and leaned over to turn off the mirror lights which were still on from the day before. As she reached for the off switch, she knocked over the mug, spilling her pens and pencils. Her journal fell to the floor and lay open face down. She picked it up, and out of curiosity, turned it over and began to read the entry.

June 7th, 2009

> *Dear Diary, today I found Mom looking at new houses on the internet. But not just looking, she was obsessive about it. Almost manic. I didn't even know she wanted to move! How long have she and Dad been talking about this? Are we moving out of Boston? Does this mean I have to leave all my friends? Ugh. Maybe that wouldn't be so awful. I am starting to feel a little trapped here. It's just so exhausting trying to live up to all these expectations. I would miss my friends, but maybe this time one of Mom's obsessions will end up being a good thing.*

As she finished reading, she looked up and was met with her tired, makeup-less face in the mirror.

"I cannot believe this is what I look like right now."

She couldn't banish the perfectionist in her so easily.

"I can't be seen like this."

She covered the dark circles under her eyes and grabbed her mascara, wanting to look presentable when they returned to the hospital. She stood nose to nose with the mirror, stroke by stroke, applying it to each eye. When she stepped back to examine herself, she sighed. She had just read an entry about wanting to be liked for who she was. Why was she still struggling with trying to be flawless? She stuffed the mascara brush back into the applicator and set it on the vanity.

"I guess this is me," she said, unconvinced.

The reflection looking back at her began melting away before her eyes. The colors faded like a watercolor painting that had been doused in water. Each stroke became a dripping streak. She touched her face and as her fingertips brushed her cheekbone, she blinked and the mirror cracked like a spider's web. Startled, she jumped back and stood there frozen. Ariel was paralyzed by the fractured reflection staring back at her.

This can't be real!

She slowly reached out her hand to touch the mirror. *This has to be a hallucination. It can't be happening.* She grazed her finger across the glass and a shard sliced the tip of her finger, drawing blood. Just as she was about to yell for her dad, she heard him calling from downstairs.

"Ariel, we have to go. Now!"

There was an urgency to his voice that frightened her. She wiped the blood off her finger and grabbed her journal, then ran downstairs. Her dad was standing at the garage door, urging her to hurry up. He was in the driver's seat before she'd even closed the passenger door.

"Dad, what's going on? Did something happen to Zach?"

His father was gripping the wheel so tightly his knuckles paled.

"No, Sweetie. Zach is okay." His voice cracked, "It's your mom."

TWENTY-THREE

IAN AND ARIEL arrived at the hospital and ran through the corridor to the nurse's station. The hospital staff had become quite fond of the family during their short time there, and recognized Ian and Ariel right away. From behind the desk, the nurse on-duty stood and pointed.

"Room Twelve." She motioned for them to keep going. They were greeted outside Room Twelve by Dr. Rapha. "Ariel, you can stay with your mom while we talk."

Her mother was asleep on the hospital bed. She ran in and bent over to hug her, but hesitated.

"It's okay," he said, using his most calming bedside manner. "You can hug her. Just be careful of the IV."

"Come with me," the doctor said.

Ian stood firm. "I want to be with my wife," he began. "Just tell me what's going on."

The doctor pointed to a glassed-in family office that was practically just across the hall from Lyana's room. "You can be with her in a moment. I just want to talk with you in private first."

Ian turned back to look in at Ariel sitting next to Lyana, holding her hand. Ariel was wiping away tears.

"Please, Mr. Keane ... Ian. It'll just be a moment. She's resting fine right now."

Ian looked over at his wife and daughter again. "I'll be back in just a couple minutes," he said. "I promise."

Ian and the doctor walked over to the private room and were joined there by one of the nurses.

The doctor nodded to the nurse, and she began to tell the story.

"I went in to check on Zach and found Lyana sobbing uncontrollably. I tried to console her, but she was unresponsive and just kept rocking back and forth with her arms in front of her, like she was holding an infant."

The nurse was speaking calmly and confidently, but it was clear to Ian that the event had shaken her.

Dr. Rapha took over. "She just kept repeating, 'Please don't leave me ... I can't lose you.' I witnessed that with my own eyes after they called me in. When our attempts to calm her failed, I authorized sedation and had her admitted to the room across the hall. We were concerned for her safety, and for Zach's. That's why I made this call. Zach needs rest. Even in his induced coma, he might hear or sense her distraught state. That would be detrimental to his healing. Has your wife been sleeping well lately?"

Ian was still trying to take it all in. "I ... I don't know. She hasn't ... Do you think it might just be exhaustion?"

"It's possible. She did appear to be a bit dehydrated, which is why she's on the saline drip, but we're concerned that this might be something a bit more complicated. We want to keep her under observation until we have more clues to go on."

Ian nodded. "Of course. That seems wise." He took a deep breath. There was no point in keeping secrets now. His wife's health was at stake. "There is something I think you should know …"

Carefully choosing his words, Ian described Lyana's episodes, where she seemed to disappear completely from the present time and become trapped in her own version of reality. "Much of the time, of course, everything is just fine and normal, but … these episodes are becoming more drawn out and more frequent, and she's disoriented and confused for a time after them."

The doctor tented his fingers and placed them on his lap. He nodded once, encouraging Ian to continue.

Ian hesitated, Lyana wasn't the only one experiencing strange things, but he was desperate to find answers. "There's more."

Dr. Rapha listened intently while Ian explained the hallucinations in as much detail as he could recall. The doctor's face remained calm and assuring, which made Ian feel at ease.

"Given what you've told me and what I saw today, I do have some thoughts on this, but before I make any judgments, I want to consult with one of my colleagues at another hospital. If he agrees with my assessment, we'll need to run some tests, including a brain scan and perhaps a spinal tap. I know this is a lot to take in right now, but I need to be honest with you. When it comes to anything related to the brain, we take things very seriously."

"You think it has something to do with her brain?"

"I'm not going to jump to conclusions. There's just not enough information. But episodes like you're describing—and the behavior we observed earlier—can indicate some kind of neurological cause."

Ian felt his world crumbling even more than it already had.

"Whatever you need to do, do it," he said.

The doctor stood and put his hand on Ian's shoulder, then walked out of the room. The nurse followed, leaving Ian alone in the small room. He grabbed his phone out of his pocket punched the call button for the newest entry on his contact list.

"Hello, Ian."

"Marshall, it looks like we're going to be here a while. Can you look after the house? I don't even remember if I locked the front door."

"Of course." There was a pause. Ian wondered if Marshall had hung up. "Did something happen to Zach?"

Ian fought to keep his voice steady. "Zach is stable. Everything is the same with him. It's Lyana. Something's wrong with Lyana."

There was another long pause before Marshall spoke again. "Don't you worry about the house. Be there for your family. And if you need anything, call."

The two hung up and Ian returned to his wife's room. Ariel was curled up on a chair next to her bed, scribbling away in her journal. He was certain she would be anxious to hear what the doctor said, but she didn't ask. She just came over and hugged him.

"I can go sit with Zach for a while," she said into his shoulder. "We should probably take turns."

"That's a good idea, Ariel. A very good idea."

Ariel gathered her travel bag and stuffed the journal inside, then walked toward the door. Just before she got there, she stopped and turned around, looking Ian right in the eye.

"Is she going to be okay?" she asked.

Ian didn't hesitate. "I'm counting on it," he said.

Ariel simply nodded, then walked through the doorway.

TWENTY-FOUR

MARSHALL BORE A striking resemblance to his uncle, and from the time he appeared at Farr Hill following his uncle's disappearance, rumors swirled around town that he was actually Mr. Goodpasture's long lost son, born to a mysterious woman he had met during one of his many adventures around the globe.

For all his time in Littleton, there was still an air of mystery to Mr. Goodpasture. He was a handsome man, captivating brown eyes, ageless olive skin. He carried himself with the kind of confidence that only comes from having experienced the great big world outside of a small eastern town. He had an innate understanding of human behavior and culture. Throughout his travels, he had collected innumerable antiquities and artifacts that, for years, decorated every available inch of his house.

He was rarely seen in town, but occasionally would grab breakfast at the café before heading to the store to pick up supplies for his next woodworking project. Several of his pieces were displayed throughout Littleton and they were stunning. They remained even after his disappearance, like a piece of him was still there watching over the town.

Plenty of rumors surrounded Mr. Goodpasture's disappearance, but the one that endured was that Mr. Goodpasture had traveled to London for an antique show and never returned. Marshall was questioned about his whereabouts through the years and his explanation never varied: his uncle had indeed traveled to London, but had a heart attack and died while he was there.

The formalities of a funeral were something Mr. Goodpasture would never have wanted.

Some townspeople believed his body was sent back to Farr Hill and that he was buried there by Marshall. Others heard he had been cremated in London and that his ashes were scattered around the property at Farr Hill.

But whatever the truth, almost from the moment of his disappearance, Marshall became the sole resident at Farr Hill.

Nobody knew much about Marshall. Like his uncle, he kept to himself and preferred the comfort of the woods to social interactions, apart from monthly trips to the grocery store or to pick up something he needed at the hardware store. His trips into town were brief and uneventful.

He was the very definition of a recluse.

Marshall had spent thirty-some years at Farr Hill, and with every passing year, his resemblance to Goodpasture became more and more apparent. He was handsome and, in his own way, kind, and while many had tried to approach him over the years, he had never taken any interest in getting married or starting a family.

As the decades passed, the stories simmered. Stories and unfounded rumors about Mr. Goodpasture would occasionally bubble up in conversation, but eventually faded into insignificance as families came and went in the quaint little town. The only people keeping the stories alive were the old timers who hung out at the "regulars" table most mornings at the café.

Little was known about Marshall, his family, or his life before Littleton. And that is exactly how *he* wanted it to be.

• • •

It was the first time he had been inside the house since the Keanes moved in.

Ian had provided him with a list of household chores to tend to and he had mentioned they left in such a rush, he was certain lights were left on throughout the house. He asked if Marshall would turn them off. He had even offered for Marshall to stay at the house while they were gone if that would make it easier for him to take care of things. Marshall politely declined.

He started in the kitchen, washing the dishes and cleaning up vegetables that had been left on the counter. He gathered up a few boxes of snacks, closed the lids, then carried them to the pantry, placing them in the open spot that looked like where they belonged.

He was captured by the remodeled pantry: the cabinets, the woodwork, the accents, and the design aesthetic. It was stunning. He stood there for a moment admiring the work, like a proud parent looking over a child's accomplishments. The only thing that remained from before was the mirror. He smiled and reached out to brush his fingers along the edges of the old mirror.

"Hello, old friend."

The wrinkles on his hand deepened, veins piercing through skin covered in age spots. He quickly removed his hand from the mirror and smirked, "I remember."

Marshall progressed up the stairs, admiring the familiar ornate carvings in the wood panels on either side on the way up. Goodpasture truly had a talent. For a moment he stopped in front of Zach's room, peering in at the hole in the wall. With a great heaviness on his heart, he stood there in silence wishing things could be different. He closed the door before heading down the hall and making his way past Ariel's bedroom to the master bedroom.

It was a beautiful room, built for comfort and functionality. The king-sized bed sat comfortably in the middle of the room; a light grey upholstered headboard and frame, layered with white, grey, and gold pillows and bedding. A small wooden bench rested at the foot of the bed, with two throw blankets folded neatly on top. To the left, positioned in front of the large window, was a sitting area complete with a loveseat, a chair, and a small table. A vase filled with still-vibrant flowers sat atop the table. Marshall bent down to breathe in their scent. Two bedside tables rested on each side of the bed, both covered with neatly stacked books. To the right was the door leading to the bathroom and another leading to the master closet. A beautiful vintage chest of drawers filled the space just on the other side of the closet door. It was a whitewashed refurbished piece, with gold hardware and etching. He ran his fingers across the surface.

Exquisite.

The lights in both the bathroom and the closet had been left on. He flipped down the switches and walked back into the bedroom. *Everything looks so different*, he thought as he scanned the room once again.

That's when he saw it.

Something in the room had cast a beautiful rainbow on the wall. He searched to find the source of the prism and saw a bright sliver of light coming from the jewelry box on top of the chest of drawers. Upon closer inspection, he discovered it was a necklace. A beautiful vintage necklace.

Marshall stood there, fixated on the necklace.

He picked it up, turning the pendant that rested in his fingertips from side to side, examining it more closely. He brought the necklace to his chest and cupped it with both hands over his heart. He closed his eyes, and whispered, "This time has to be the last."

TWENTY-FIVE

ZACH REMAINED IN the hospital for over a week. He was in a coma for five days and stayed another five for monitoring. His vitals were showing signs of continued improvement and the swelling throughout his body had gone down substantially. The doctors were elated that the brain scans showed no signs of damage. They assured Ian that Zach would likely make a full recovery.

It was the best news Ian could have received.

"If all goes well for the next twenty-four hours, he will be able to go home soon." Dr. Rapha's enthusiasm was hard to miss. Things had been so dire that first night, and now they were mere hours away from bringing Zach home.

But Ian couldn't exhale fully quite yet. They still didn't have any explanation for Lyana's episodes.

She hadn't left the hospital. After spending that first night in her own room, under the supervision of the nurses, she returned to Zach's side. She was there day and night, caring for him, seemingly recovered from whatever it was that had sent her over the edge before. She wanted to stay close should anything happen. After several days, nurses tried to convince her that some fresh air and a shower from the comfort of home would do wonders for her, but she told Ian she couldn't

155

fathom leaving Zach alone in that hospital. She showered in the hospital room instead while Ian watched over Zach.

Many people had come and gone over the days, including a surprising number of kids from school dropping off cards they had made and checking in. While Zach was still in a coma, Lyana would read the cards to him, hoping he could hear how many people cared for him. Once he woke up, she read them to him again.

Ian and Ariel tried to resume some aspects of life, like work and school. Ian had sensed Ariel's frustration with the dramatic change to her routine, and even though he knew she agreed to stay at the hospital during Zach's recovery, he gave her the occasional reprieve—some time at home to get a taste of normality amid the chaos.

Throughout the whole ordeal, Lloyd and his café staff provided meals almost every day Zach remained in the hospital. It was a small silver lining in the storm they had been enduring.

Ian set the warm food containers on the seat next to him while he was parked next to the café. He smiled and mouthed a "thank you" at Lloyd, who was waving at him from behind the wide front window. He turned to survey the street in front of him. He saw three signs in storefront windows that nearly brought him to tears.

Get Well, Zach
You Got This, Zach!
We love you, Zach!

Tragedy has a way of bringing people together, he thought to himself. Seeing the locals surround them with support made Ian see Littleton in a completely new light. When he told Lyana about the signs, she gasped with a rare moment of delight, then hugged Ian tightly.

For the first time in their adult life, Ian and Lyana had a village of people around them. And despite all the strangeness at Farr Hill, Ian knew without a doubt that they hadn't just stumbled upon a house.

They'd found home.

TWENTY-SIX

ONE YEAR EARLIER
Winter was one of her favorite times of the year in Boston and like many winters before, Lyana would often find herself strolling through the gardens. The tree-lined Freedom Trail was beautifully lit, a golden hue glistening off the bare branches onto the snow. Her strolls would typically bring her to Faneuil Hall, where she would grab something to eat before finding a bench along the trail to people watch and clear her head.

Sitting in the cold never really bothered her. She enjoyed the brisk air—it was a welcome departure from the hot Kentucky summers she grew up with.

Lyana could sit there for hours—reflecting on life, creating music, or just taking it all in. Boston was ethereal in the winter, and it really was the perfect place for their family. It fed Ian's love for history, and the university there presented him with so many meaningful opportunities. The music scene was also vibrant and inspiring, giving Lyana just as many reasons to love Boston as Ian.

The kids loved Boston as much as their parents, but on that December day it was the kids she was worried about. They had become restless in the city. She hoped the brisk air and outdoor time would help her gain clarity on the recent changes in their demeanor.

Zach always had a hard time making friends, but had recently been the target of a group of bullies, the same group his sister was spending more and more time with. The incident created a rift between the two of them, and although Lyana and Ian tried to explain to Ariel that her new friends were reflecting poorly on her, she wouldn't believe them, despite what had happened with Zach.

At home, Ariel was always so kind and compassionate. She was naturally an introvert, but could *turn it on* when needed. It was a skill. Lyana had recently begun to notice Ariel's true nature, getting lost in putting on a show anytime she was around others, and it concerned her. It seemed her daughter was trying to be someone or something she was not simply to fit in with the "in" crowd. Lyana knew from experience changing that path would be a painful journey, but despite Lyana's pleas, Ariel was going to do whatever she wanted. Lyana knew she had to let go and allow Ariel to make her own choices. She just hoped Ariel would eventually realize her parents were only trying to help, and that they were there for her all along.

Giving Ariel the freedom to choose her own path was difficult, and while Lyana was holding it together at home, she wasn't quite so successful putting on a brave face when she was alone. Thankfully, the long walks and time sitting on benches breathing in the redolent scents of the garden gave her an opportunity to put everything into perspective. Being a parent could feel so lonely sometimes, constantly wondering if she was making the right choices for her family. Lyana often felt like she carried the weight of the family on her shoulders; she wanted to fix everything for everyone. Still, she knew she couldn't protect them forever, as much as her heart ached to.

It was an unusually warm day for December with temps in the mid-fifties. Lyana sat on her favorite bench, her army green puffer jacket zipped midway up her chest, open just enough to show the off-white sweater she was wearing. She didn't need a scarf on this day, but still wore her Dubarry boots and her favorite trapper hat. She removed her gloves so she could pick up the sandwich she had just purchased from the deli. The butcher paper was open and resting on her lap as an impromptu table, and as she picked up the sandwich to take a bite, she was interrupted.

"Is this seat taken?"

He was an older gentleman. His eyes were kind and asserted a quiet confidence. There was something about him that reminded Lyana of her own grandfather, or perhaps of someone else she had met before, but she couldn't place it. The more she tried to focus on his face, the less she could pinpoint any details.

"No, you're welcome to sit," she offered in response. He sat.

He was dressed nicely, wearing a dark blue topcoat, scarf, and thin tan gloves. The greys of his once dark hair were almost white under the tree lights. His jaw was shadowed by a slight scruff, like maybe he hadn't shaved for a few days. He looked well put together, like a businessman.

Lyana was curious about the man beside her. She sensed he had a story, but she didn't want to pry, so she took another bite of her sandwich.

"What brings you out on this beautiful day?" he asked as she chewed the delicious sandwich. She quietly noted the deli as another reason she loved Boston.

There was something familiar and comfortable about the man, so she didn't hesitate to engage in conversation.

"I come here a lot," she said after swallowing the bit of her sandwich. "The park benches are the perfect place to pause, you know? To think about life and maybe seek clarity about … things."

"What sort of things are on your heart today?"

Without hesitation, she began describing the recent challenges with the kids, but she didn't stop there. She talked about what brought her and Ian to Boston, and even shared some of their struggles. The words just rolled off her tongue. The man's captivating presence made it easy to talk.

After a few minutes, she stopped. "I'm sorry," she said. "I'm talking your ear off." She looked down at her mostly uneaten sandwich.

"No, no. It's no trouble. I welcome the conversation. Your family sounds wonderful."

He listened as she opened like a flood gate, sharing personal details of their life and struggles, and why the current situation was heavily weighing on her heart. He hung on to every word she spoke. She was surprised by his undevoted attention, and by her own openness. She hadn't been this vulnerable with anyone before, apart from her sister.

At one point her voice cracked as she spoke of her children. For comfort, she reached deep into the pocket of her coat and pulled out her grandmother's necklace. She held it in her hand as she continued to tell this strange yet gentle man everything.

"What's that in your hand, dear?"

Lyana loosened her grip and revealed the necklace. The chain slipped between two of her fingers and the pendant lay there resting and on display in the middle of her hand. As the sunshine danced across the surface, it animated vibrant colors over the midnight stone.

"It was my grandmother's."

The man nodded. "It's quite lovely," he said.

"I always carry it with me, for guidance and comfort."

She told him how her grandmother had given it to her just before she and Ian left for Boston after graduation. It had been passed down from generation to generation, and her grandmother insisted she carry it with her to never forget her strength or where she came from. It was a constant reminder that the answers were always close. "Sometimes we just need to be willing to see and hear them," her grandmother would say.

He looked at it curiously. "It really is a beautiful piece. I can understand why it means so much to you."

Lyana glanced at her watch. *How the time has passed!* "This has been really lovely. Thank you so much for listening. You are a very patient man." She laughed at herself, then began wrapping the mostly uneaten sandwich for later.

"Do you mind if I give you some advice?" he asked.

His tone wasn't the least bit demanding or arrogant, and at this point, she was open to any and all suggestions. She knew she didn't have all the answers and that was exactly why she had taken the time to come to the park.

"Sometimes a change of scenery is exactly what a person needs," he offered.

She offered a sheepish smile back, along with a raised eyebrow. She and Ian had talked about the possibility of moving in passing over the last few weeks, but it wasn't anything either had considered seriously. They certainly hadn't shared the thought with anyone else.

"Well, I best be on my way." The man stood, nodded politely at her, and turned to walk away.

"Thank you," she called after him. She realized in that moment she hadn't even learned his name.

She decided she had a little more time and went back to eating her sandwich, playing his words over and over in her head. *A change of scenery.* When she looked up not a minute later, the man was nowhere in sight. She smiled to herself, gripping the necklace in her hand, then let out a faint giggle. She put the necklace back in her pocket and finished eating.

The man's words stayed with her for months.

She would often sit up at night, wondering if he was right. She started being more intentional, talking with Ian about the possibility of moving. He seemed open to the idea, but nothing had propelled them to act on it.

As the winter snow began to melt and the season changed from spring to summer, at the end of the school year Zach experienced yet another bullying incident brought on by Ariel's friends. Lyana was at her wits end.

It was June.

Lyana sat in the darkened living room sipping a glass of wine searching through real estate listings. She didn't have any idea what she was looking for, or even where to look. She was just so frustrated by the current situation with the kids she wanted an escape. *Then again*, she thought, *maybe something will pop up anyway.*

Something did catch her attention.

In Littleton, New Hampshire. She'd never heard of the town.

Lyana clicked on the listing and began scrolling through pictures. She read the description, looked at the pictures a second time, and then a third. She opened another browser and did a map search to see how far away Littleton was from Boston. She sat up in her chair, studying all that stared back at her from the computer screen.

"Mom, what's that?"

Lyana jumped, startled by Ariel's sudden presence.

"Sorry, I didn't notice you come in the room," she said. "Take a look at this," she said, scooting to the side so Ariel could join her at the computer.

Lyana clicked through the pictures and read the description aloud.

"Wait," Ariel said. "Are we really thinking of moving?"

Lyana wasn't sure how to respond. But she didn't need to.

"It looks awesome," said Ariel. The excitement in her voice was palpable.

"Really?" Lyana was shocked by her response. She had braced herself for an argument and for Ariel to present all the reasons they shouldn't move. Instead, Ariel actually seemed excited about the possibility.

"Yeah. Maybe a change of scenery would be good for me. For all of us." Ariel gave her mother a quick side hug, then skipped away, likely to go add another entry to her journal.

A change of scenery. That was exactly how the stranger had worded it. *Was a change of scenery exactly what they needed? How would Zach respond to something new?*

She picked up her phone to text Ian who was in Germany giving a lecture. She couldn't contain her excitement. After hitting send, she called the realtor from the listing to schedule a viewing for the weekend after Ian returned from overseas.

TWENTY-SEVEN

IAN BEGAN GATHERING the flowers and cards from the hospital room to carry them to the car that was parked at the front of the hospital. Ariel was packing the travel bags, while the nurses and Lyana were situating Zach in the wheelchair they would use to take him to the car.

"Can't say I'm gonna miss this place," Zach said to the nurse who had helped him into the chair. She gently punched his arm.

"Well, I don't blame ya, but we're going to miss you." The nurse looked over at Ian. "That said, I don't wanna see any of you around here for a long while. Capiche?"

"I don't know what capiche means," said Zach, "but I'm all for staying away."

He was back to his clever, fun self. He'd lost a little weight and was just a little unsteady on his feet, but Zach was back. Ian was infinitely thankful for that.

He made one final trip to the car, then joined the rest of the family and the discharge nurse in the room for one final goodbye to this place.

Dr. Rapha and a handful of staff greeted them and cheered as they made their way through the hallway and to the elevator. Zach was beaming with pride. For someone who often struggled when he was the center of attention, he was relishing it in this moment.

"You all take care now," said Dr. Rapha.

Zach offered the doc a fist bump, saying "You got it, doc," before holding up his left hand and collecting high fives from all the staff members who lined the hallway. It was clear to Ian that everyone there had come to love Zach and their entire family.

As the elevator door opened, Ian turned to his family, "I'll meet you downstairs." The door closed and he walked swiftly back to the nurses' station, where Dr. Rapha was still standing. Extending a hand, he said, "Thank you again for everything."

"Of course. It was my pleasure." The doctor gripped Ian's hand and held it for an extra beat, offering a look of support and concern. "I will be in touch soon."

Ian nodded and walked back to the elevator. He changed his mind and headed for the stairs, deciding the extra few minutes to reflect, and the aerobic exercise, would be good for him.

He was slightly out of breath when he reached the car. "Alright guys," he said excitedly, "Let's blow this popsicle stand!"

An excited chorus of "Yes!" reverberated in the car. It felt like it had been months since the accident. Ian knew everyone couldn't wait to get back to their home, their own beds, to familiarity.

As they drove down main street, it was like they were the lead float in a parade. Balloons floated from street signs and people cheered from the sidewalks. New homemade signs had replaced the earlier ones, these offering words such as, *Congrats, Zach.*

"Can you believe this?" Lyana said.

"It's a lot, don't you think?" offered Ariel. She sounded more incredulous than jealous.

"It's amazing!" shouted Zach. "I'm famous!" He started counting the people who were lining the road. "27, 28 …"

Lloyd waved from the sidewalk just in front of the café. He had visited Zach in the hospital every day, usually bringing along food. When Zach was out of his coma, Lloyd would sit and talk with him for what seemed like hours. He had assured Ian he'd continue to provide meals for the first week when everyone was back. "Then you'll have to come in and pay me like normal people" Lloyd had added, with a sly smile.

Ian rolled down the window and yelled to Lloyd, "This your idea?" He pointed to the crowd.

Lloyd just smiled one of his trademark smiles and shrugged.

Ian called out again, "Five o'clock?"

Lloyd held up a thumbs up and shouted back, "See you then!"

"Dad, turn on some music," said Zach.

Ian started scrolling through radio stations and turned up the volume as a familiar piano melody rang out.

He said, "Son when you grow up,
Would you be the savior of the broken,
The beaten and the damned?"

Without prompting, all four of them began to sing in one voice, as loudly as they could.

He said "Will you defeat them?
Your demons, and all the non-believers
The plans that they have made?"
"Because one day, I'll leave you a phantom,
To lead you in the summer
To join the black parade."

Ian began drumming on the steering wheel, Zach picked up his air guitar and with precision, mimed the epic guitar solo. Lyana and Ariel began dancing and banging their heads as if they were enjoying front row seats at a concert.

While Lyana was classically trained, she had a secret passion for Pop Punk and Emo music. She was always introducing the kids—and sometimes Ian—to new songs and bands. Ian loved that about her. *My Chemical Romance* was one of her favorites. Their lyrics felt spiritual, transcendent, and powerful.

To carry on, we'll carry on
And though you're dead and gone, believe me
Your memory will carry on

They continued to sing, splitting off into harmony while playing their instruments, then shouting at the top of their lungs each time the chorus came around.

By the time the song ended there was a palpable feeling of hope and elation in the car. It had been a long time since the whole family had sung and laughed with one another. This, thought Ian, was pure joy. They had needed this for a long time.

When they arrived at home, it looked like they hadn't even been gone. Marshall had kept the house in pristine condition, so they didn't have to worry about a thing. He had even taken the time to fix the hole in Zach's room.

Marshall wasn't there when they arrived.

Ariel and Ian had been going back and forth between the house and the hospital, so the return home wasn't as shocking to them as it was to Zach and Lyana. The two of them stood in the kitchen and embraced, while Ian and Ariel gathered everything from the car and brought it in.

• • •

"I am so glad you are home, sweetheart," said Lyana, reluctant to let go of Zach.

"Me, too." Zach struggled a little in Lyana's grasp. "Um, you can let go now, Mom."

She disengaged from the hug and held his face in her hands instead, then kissed his forehead.

The two of them walked hand in hand up the stairs. Lyana knew the return likely would be difficult for him. She didn't want to leave his side.

"… 13, 14, 15." Zach let out a sigh of relief. Ian and Ariel were waiting for them outside his room. The door was closed.

Ariel stepped back as Lyana and Ian stood on either side of Zach, hooking arms with him as they opened the door to his room. They all stood there, letting everything sink in.

The room looked like nothing had happened. Marshall had done an excellent job with the wall repair, but all the paint and drywall in the world couldn't erase the memory of what had occurred.

Zach slipped out of his parents' arms and walked over to examine the wall. He ran his fingers across the surface, then turned to his parents. "I'm okay, you guys."

"Are you sure?" asked Lyana.

"I'm sure," he reiterated.

"Well, you know we're nearby if you need anything," added Ian. "We will be in our room unpacking."

Ian walked out of the room first. Lyana followed behind but paused in the doorway to look back at Zach. He smiled and motioned for her to keep going.

"I'm fine," he said again.

She was still apprehensive, but knew he needed to process the entire event his own way.

Once in their room, Lyana fell backward onto the bed and let out a sigh that was full of all the emotion she'd stored up in the last several weeks. As she sat up, contemplating whether she should unpack or just rest for a moment, she remembered that she had left her necklace at home. She had forgotten to grab it when they were heading to the hospital. She had been a complete mess, then, singularly focused on Zach and his recovery.

Ian was talking to her from the closet as he was unpacking, but she could hardly hear what he was saying and simply responded with an "uh huh" every now and then, signaling she was engaged in whatever it was he was saying.

She stood and moved to the dresser. The necklace was exactly where she left it. She held the pendant in her hands for a moment, then put it on and closed her eyes, simply breathing for a moment.

"Mom?" She opened her eyes. Zach was standing in the doorway.

"Yeah, Zach?" Ian heard him come into their room and peeked his head out from the closet door.

"You good?" Ian asked.

"Dad, can we go downstairs and just watch a movie or something?"

"Of course we can." Ian dropped what he was doing in the closet. "Is this an all-family event?"

Zach paused. "How about just us boys for now?"

Lyana was happy to let Zach and Ian have some time together. She had been by his side for weeks.

"You boys enjoy. I have some stuff to do." She was eager to check on her vegetable garden.

Lyana followed the boys out of the room, pausing at Ariel's door to see she was lying on her bed, scribbling away in her journal. She didn't look up.

TWENTY-EIGHT

L LOYD HAD JUST turned onto the driveway to Farr Hill when he saw Lyana. She was turning around and around in circles. He popped his truck into park and jumped out and jogged over to her. She was stumbling and mumbling something under her breath. It sounded like a foreign language, but Lloyd couldn't place it.

"Mrs. Keane, are you okay?"

She wasn't wearing shoes or a coat. His attempts to get her to walk to his car were unsuccessful, so he picked her up. She kept talking gibberish, like she was lost in her own world.

He moved the food from the passenger seat into the back and carefully placed her in the truck to bring her home.

As he approached the house, he began honking the horn.

• • •

Ian looked out the window and spotted Lloyd's truck arriving but wasn't sure why he was honking or driving so fast. "Zach, stay here."

Ian got up from the kitchen table and went to see what all the commotion was about. He went through the garage and as he hit the button to open the double garage door, Lloyd was standing at the passenger side of his truck, pulling Lyana out. He picked her up in his arms.

"What happened?" Ian ran to help.

"I found her up the driveway like this."

"We need to get her inside."

Ian and Lloyd shouldered Lyana between them and practically carried her up the stairs to the bedroom. Ian laid her down on the bed as gently as he could. She was still staring off into space and mumbling incoherently.

"I'll stay with her. Can you go check on the kids?"

Lloyd nodded and walked out of the room.

Ian sat on the side of the bed, unsure how to help Lyana. He started rubbing her back.

"Be with me," he said, practically in a whisper. She didn't respond, but after a couple minutes, she settled down. Her breathing relaxed and Ian thought she must have fallen asleep.

Ian went downstairs to find Lloyd in the kitchen, setting the table for the dinner he'd brought.

"Zach seems fine," Lloyd said. "Didn't see Ariel, yet." He pointed at the stairs. "How is Lyana?"

"I think I managed to get her settled down. She's resting now."

He knew Lloyd would have more questions, so without going into too many details he explained that Lyana had been having these episodes for a while now and that she had even had one while in the hospital.

"When the doctors saw her in that state, they wanted to run a few tests. I thought I'd have heard something by now, but … soon, I think."

He excused himself to go check on Zach.

"Hey kiddo." Zach was still resting on the couch, watching the movie. "You want to come get some dinner in the kitchen? Mr. Warner brought your favorite."

"Is Mom okay?"

"She's resting."

"Who's resting?" Ariel chimed in as she walked into the kitchen.

"Your mother."

"Why, is something up?" she asked.

"Your mom was just exhausted, that's all. These past couple of weeks have been hard on her."

Ariel shrugged. "Okay."

Zach slid into his seat at the table. "I'm starving. Let's eat!"

Ariel sat down and Ian noticed Lloyd had only set three places.

"Aren't you going to join us?" Ian asked.

"Yeah, please do," added Zach. "Please!"

"Thanks, but I should be heading home. You all enjoy your meal." He had started to head toward the door when Ariel chimed in.

"Please, we insist."

Lloyd stopped and turned around, offering a thankful smile. "Well, in that case. I suppose I can stay for a little while."

Ian had just cut into his stack of fluffy pancakes drenched in local maple syrup when the phone rang. He excused himself from the table to answer the call.

"This is Ian."

"Ian, it's Dr. Rapha."

This was the call he had been waiting for. Anxiety and anticipation swelled.

"I'd rather talk about this in person, Ian. It's complicated. Could you come to the office tomorrow?"

The two set an appointment for nine o'clock the next morning. Ian knew it couldn't be good.

TWENTY-NINE

T HE NEXT MORNING as Ian made the drive from Farr Hill to Dr. Rapha's office, his thoughts were all over the map. He teetered from hope to tears, swinging the pendulum between the worst-case scenario and the best possible outcome. He had heard it before, *it's always bad news when the Doctor needs to see you in person,* and knew he needed to use the time during the drive to prepare himself for whatever was coming.

The sinking feeling in the pit of his stomach told him everything he needed to know, but he couldn't let his mind stay in that dark place. Lyana was everything to him and the thought of something being seriously wrong was simply too much to comprehend. And the thought of losing her? He thought about all their years together and the life they had worked hard to build. All the obstacles they'd overcome. He didn't know life without her.

This was supposed to be our fresh start.

The words rolled off his tongue as he pulled into the parking garage. He turned off the car and sat for a minute, collecting himself. He wiped a stray tear from his cheek and took a deep breath before getting out of the car. The walk from his car to Dr. Rapha's office felt like an eternity.

With each step, another stray thought. It took everything within him to keep moving toward that office door. Part of him wanted to run in the other direction and pretend everything was just fine. But he needed to know. He needed to face this.

He couldn't help but think of Lyana on their wedding day, walking toward him in that simple, understated white dress, vowing to spend forever together. She was stunning, her hair pulled back slightly off her face. He felt like the luckiest man alive. She had been his best friend since they were kids and he always assumed they would grow old together.

He took a deep breath, then opened the door.

"Take a seat, the doctor will be right with you." The nurse behind the check-in desk directed him to one of the chairs in the empty waiting area.

The wait was excruciating. Ian fidgeted, clasping his hands together and rubbing his knuckles. His leg was shaking ever so slightly, and he kept switching positions every few minutes for comfort. He was a wreck.

"Ian," Dr. Rapha reached out with a handshake.

Ian followed him to his office, then the door closed behind them. Dr. Rapha motioned to one of the two chairs that sat in front of his desk before sitting down in his own dark leather office chair. The room was full of pictures of his family, and several framed degrees hung on the wall. Two dark cherry wood bookshelves were lined with medical books. Ian kept looking around, avoiding eye contact.

"There is no easy way to say this."

Ian's eyes met the doctor's.

"We wanted to be sure." Dr. Rapha was calm in his delivery. "It's Lewy Body Dementia."

Ian heard the words, but it took him a minute to process them. He had prepared himself for the worst possible news, but he had assumed it was cancer or something along those lines.

"Dementia? But, how? Lyana is young. Dementia is something old people get, right? There has to be a mistake." It was incomprehensible.

Dr. Rapha was empathetic as he explained that this type of dementia was extremely progressive, more so than Alzheimer's, and that it sometimes afflicted younger adults. Ian didn't want to believe this was happening, but as the doctor described the early stages and its progression—the hallucinations, the confusion, the memory loss, the blurred line between what was real and what wasn't—it all started to make some sense.

"There is more."

How could there be more? Ian was taking it all in, but it was so much to try to process. He listened intently as the doctor continued. Because of Lyana's age, Dr. Rapha wanted to speak to Ian first before bringing her in to discuss the condition, but he also knew they had a limited amount of time because of the rapid progression of the disease.

"I have never seen it happen this fast or with someone so young," he added.

Ian couldn't help but think of what this would do to Lyana. Losing her memories, slowly becoming unrecognizable. He knew enough about dementia to understand how she would change mentally, but he struggled to digest Dr. Rapha's explanation that she would lose motor skills and physical abilities as well, leaving her a prisoner in her own body. He called the condition Locked-in Syndrome. She would have awareness of her surroundings and lucid moments, but no ability to move or speak.

"Cherish the moments you have now."

His sentiments angered Ian, but the anger quickly turned to sadness, and he broke down. Sitting hunched over, his face buried in his hands, he couldn't believe what he was hearing. Their *forever* now had an expiration date.

"How are we going to tell her? How am I going to explain this to the kids?" His thoughts started racing again.

Dr. Rapha assured him they would get through it together. The two of them made a plan. Ian and Lyana would come back later that day. Dr. Rapha would arrange to have a support counselor present should they want to talk about how to discuss the diagnosis with the kids. They would explain to Lyana the progression of the disease and what to expect in the coming weeks and months.

"I'm truly sorry, Ian. I really am."

The doctor escorted him all the way to the elevator, offering a supportive pat on the shoulder.

Ian walked back to the car in a fog.

The drive from Dr. Rapha's office back to Farr Hill felt like it took forever, and yet not long enough. He dreaded the next few hours. And he couldn't help but think how all of this was soon to be a distant memory for his wife. *What would she remember? Would she forget him? Would she forget their children? How long would they have with her until her mind erased everything?*

As he pulled into the driveway, Coldplay's "Fix You" came on the radio. He listened as he inched closer to the house.

And the tears come streaming down your face
When you lose something you can't replace
Lights will guide you home
And ignite your bones
And I will try to fix you

The words pierced him, the truth sitting on his chest like a dead weight. The garage door began to open. Just beyond that door was his family who had no idea what they were about to face.

The song trailed to a finish, and he turned the ignition off. He had to hold it together and couldn't let on that he knew anything until the doctor had a chance to talk to Lyana and the two of them could figure out how to tell the kids. He wanted to shut himself away and be swallowed whole by his emotions, but his family was going to need him. He needed to be strong.

"Hey, Dad. Take a look at this." Zach and Ariel were sitting together in the kitchen, working on a puzzle she had received the Christmas before. Ian couldn't remember the last time he saw the two of them working on a puzzle together.

They were about a third of the way toward completing the 1,000-piece flowing rainbow puzzle. The island countertop was dusted with crumbs from the donuts the two had eaten for breakfast.

"How'd it go in town?" Ariel barely looked up when she spoke. Zach was completely immersed in the puzzle and didn't even acknowledge Ian's arrival.

He had told them he needed to see Dr. Rapha for some follow-up treatment information for Zach and that it would be a quick trip. They would know the harsh truth soon enough.

"It was fine," he said. *It was the opposite of fine.* "Where's your mom?" As soon as the words left Ian's mouth, Lyana came into the kitchen, an extra skip in her step and a smile from ear to ear, like nothing had happened the night before. Ian swallowed the lump in his throat and looked at her. She looked radiant. Maybe the doctor got it wrong. Maybe they misdiagnosed her. Lyana was standing in front of him as vibrant as she was the day he married her.

None of it made any sense.

He leaned over and kissed her cheek, "Ly, can we talk for a minute?" She gave him a puzzled look, but nodded. He took her by the hand and led her to his study. The kids didn't look up as they walked away.

Once they were safely out of ear shot of the kids and the study door was closed, Ian sat Lyana down and began telling her about his meeting with the Dr. Rapha.

"Do you remember those tests you took at the hospital?"

The question clearly took her by surprise. Her smile slowly faded. She nodded.

"We need to go back to the hospital to talk with him."

"When?"

"In just a few hours," he said. Ian took a deep breath. He knew what was coming next. His wife wouldn't leave it at that.

"What did he tell you?" The joy he had seen in her eyes just a few moments earlier was completely gone now.

Ian wanted to tell her everything but knew he couldn't. Reluctantly, he lied.

"That's all I know." He convinced her that his meeting earlier was in fact to discuss Zach, but that her tests had come up in conversation and the doctor wanted to see them both to discuss what they'd found. He gave no indication that he knew what was coming and she trusted he was telling her the truth.

It was crushing for Ian. He had never lied to his wife, but he knew he couldn't do this alone and needed Dr. Rapha to be the one to tell her. How could he look at his wife and tell her that soon she would forget him, their life, all the memories? That their children would become strangers occupying space in the same house, a house that would also feel unfamiliar. The hardest part to think about was the combination of Lewy Body with Locked-in Syndrome. Even Dr. Rapha struggled to explain how they might work against her in tandem. It was a medical anomaly, particularly for someone her age.

Ian had called Lloyd on his way home and asked if he could come over to be at the house with the kids while he and Lyana met with Dr. Rapha. The kids were certainly old enough to stay on their own, but knowing what was coming and what they had all just walked through with Zach, the thought of leaving them alone unsettled him. They would be in good hands with Lloyd. Lloyd was the only other person who knew about Lyana's tests and was happy to help.

Lyana was upstairs getting ready while the kids remained in the kitchen working on the puzzle. Ian sat down and joined them, picking up a few pieces and searching intently for where they belonged. He nonchalantly mentioned to the kids that they needed to go back into town for a few things and that Mr. Warner was going to come and stay with them.

Zach smiled and went back to concentrating on the puzzle.

"I am too old for a babysitter," Ariel complained, but she didn't push it. "But that's fine. Maybe he'll bring some of that delicious, sugared bacon."

When Lloyd arrived, he and Ian exchanged a look. Ian glanced over at the kids and saw Zach looking directly at them. His expression was unreadable.

"I think I need a break," Zach said. He put down the piece he had been working on and let out a sigh. "I could use a nap."

Ariel shrugged and stopped working on the puzzle too. She looked up at Lloyd. "You didn't happen to bring any tasty food, did you?"

"I'm sorry, no. I didn't. But I can make something for you here if you like."

"Okay. Popcorn, then. I'm gonna watch a movie." She left the kitchen and headed to the living room.

Lloyd turned to Ian and Lyana, "Popcorn?"

Lyana pointed. "It's in the pantry."

Ian mouthed a "thank you" to Lloyd, then led Lyana into the garage, closing the door behind them.

THIRTY

*L*EWY BODY DEMENTIA.

Lyana couldn't believe what she was hearing.

Ian held her hand as he sat next to her in the doctor's office.

She was only thirty-six-years old. It was unbelievable and shocking. She looked over at Ian, but he had his head in his hands.

"Doctor, with all due respect, there must be a mistake," she insisted.

Dr. Rapha explained that he had consulted with several of his colleagues because he, too, found it hard to believe himself and there was so much about her diagnosis that left him perplexed. He had been in the medical field for thirty years and had never seen anything like it.

Calmly, Ian asked, "What happens next?"

Lyana looked over at him, her eyes wide with shock.

"How can you ask that? How can you just trust that this is all true? You're not fighting it!" She turned to the doctor. "We'll get a second opinion." Then back to Ian. "Tell him we need a second opinion, Ian!"

Ian opened his mouth to speak, but just then there was a knock at the door. A woman in her forties entered and leaned against the doctor's desk, offering a gentle, if forced smile.

"This is Shelly Lewis," the doctor said. "I've asked her to join us because she's experienced at helping families work through difficult medical circumstances such as this."

It all sounded so rehearsed to Lyana. She was still wondering why Ian hadn't agreed with her about getting a second opinion. And upset that he had lied to her.

"Why don't you take a moment," the counselor said. "This is a lot to take in."

Lyana jumped out of her chair, not saying a word to anyone. She brushed past Ian without making eye contact and swiftly headed to the bathroom. He got up and followed but by the time he caught up, the bathroom door was swinging closed.

She thought she might throw up, but the feeling passed. She leaned back against the bathroom wall and slid down to the floor, pulling her arms around her knees and burying her head in them. A single word echoed in her head: *Why?*

In time, she'd cried herself out. She stood, splashed water on her face, then walked out into the hallway.

Ian reached out his arms to hug her. She refused the gesture and walked right past him, then stopped suddenly and faced him.

"How dare you keep this from me? You knew!"

"Please, Ly, let me explain …"

"You lied to me!"

"What choice did I have?"

"Have you been lying about anything else?" She practically shouted.

Ian looked totally shocked. "Have I … what? No. I promise."

She sat down on a chair just outside Dr. Rapha's office and buried her head in her hands. Ian knelt and placed his hands on her knees and explained everything. She heard all his words, but none of them eased the pain. It just wasn't fair.

"How are we going to tell the kids?" She started to cry again and leaned into Ian's extended arms. After a few more minutes, she stood up and Ian led her back to Dr. Rapha's office where the four or them discussed that very thing. The thought of her children without a mother was unbearable. And she shuddered at the thought of them seeing her as a shell of herself.

Lyana declined Ms. Lewis's offer to tell the kids about the diagnosis and decided it would be best for her and Ian to deliver the news to Zach and Ariel on their own. She said they would feel betrayed if they heard the news from someone else.

Ms. Lewis expressed concern that this would be a lot for the Keane children to take in and reiterated that she would be there to help walk them through everything. Dr. Rapha also reminded them that he was only a phone call away.

The car ride home was silent. Somber.

Lyana barely said two words to Ian. She was still frustrated with him for not telling her the truth earlier. She understood his reasons, but it certainly didn't make her feel any better.

Doctor Rapha had gently explained before they left that they had essentially gotten more than one second opinion on the diagnosis, since the condition was so unexpected, and so rare. The doctor had seen to that himself, just to be sure.

The diagnosis certainly explained the episodes, the visions, and feelings of confusion, but there were still so many unanswered questions.

"I'm sorry," Ian said quietly as he reached over and grabbed her hand.

"I know," she replied.

Ian opened the garage door and pulled the car inside.

THIRTY-ONE

I T HAD BEEN almost a month since Ian and Lyana shared the news with Zach and Ariel. A day that would forever be etched in their memories. The before and after moment for their family. Up until then, Lyana's episodes had remained a mystery and while abnormal, they were brushed off and chalked up to exhaustion or lack of sleep. Now, not only was there a diagnosis but there was a sense of fear knowing what was ahead.

They were forced to face the harsh reality of Lyana's mortality.

Lyana was the glue that kept the family together, and the thought of doing any of it without her was excruciating.

Ian observed that each of them was processing the news in different ways.

Ariel had been so helpful in the days following Zach's homecoming. The two of them had never been closer. They were spending so much time together, working on puzzles or watching movies. Ian believed it was the one good thing that had come of all this, but upon learning the news of her mother's illness, Ariel admitted that she felt lost and alone. The idea of losing anyone in her family was too much for her. She began isolating herself in her room, leaning even more heavily on the solace that her journal provided. Ian knew that her words made her feel safe and that's where she hid out when the news of her mother landed with a resounding thud in her lap.

Meanwhile, Zach was laser-focused on piecing everything together. He picked up exactly where he left off before the attack. The attack hadn't shaken his feeling that there was more to all that was happening, and now he was convinced it was all somehow connected. He was determined to get to the bottom of it.

The day he learned of his mother's illness, he made a promise to her.

"Mom, I don't care what it takes, I am going to figure this out."

When Ian heard this, it put a knot in his throat. Zach was so sure of himself, so certain he could find an answer to this impossible situation. But Ian didn't say anything. If Zach needed hope to keep going, he wasn't going to pop that bubble.

Dr. Rapha and Ms. Lewis came to the house the day after the kids got the news to talk with all of them and answer any questions they might have. Since then, Zach and Ariel had met with Ms. Lewis and had been talking with her regularly. So had Ian. But even with the additional support, it was devastating. No one knew how long they had with her or when the good moments—or the bad—were coming.

Even in that short amount of time, the disease was showing signs of taking over. Lyana's episodes continued to increase in frequency and duration.

Dr. Rapha's words kept replaying in Ian's head— "Cherish the moments that you have." He was doing his best to make the most of those moments, but it was so hard.

There were times he would look across the room and see the Lyana he had married, so vibrant and full of life. And then there were other moments when she would sit staring off in the distance, trapped by her own thoughts or frozen by her inability to move.

Ian dealt with the news by diving into the one place where he always felt comfortable: History. He would sit in his study, reading book after book. Some of that time he was trying to learn everything he could about dementia and locked-in syndrome, but he also welcomed the distraction of folding himself into a good history book. And even a historical novel or two. He deliberately avoided having anything to do with alcohol, despite the temptation of the half-empty bottle still sitting on the shelf.

The nuances of the house that once felt charming to Ian were now a focal point for exploration as he, not unlike Zach, tried to piece together the historical significance of their home. He spent hours lost in books, trying to forget the reality that he was losing his wife to a horrific disease. Trying, but failing.

Lyana dealt with her diagnosis with tenacity. She wasn't about to allow any disease to diminish her—at least not as long as she was lucid and able to engage in "normal" life. She was also comforted knowing that Zach sensed the same things she did and that what she was feeling about this house—about how this story they were living wasn't part of her diagnosis.

From the minute she arrived at Farr Hill, something had been pulling at her, infiltrating her thoughts—an invisible force guiding her. But it had become difficult for her to know what was real and what wasn't. She felt like she was always playing a mind game. Was she thinking clearly about things or was this just more evidence of the steadily growing dementia?

Those long, often meandering conversations with Zach gave her assurance, like all was not lost in the abyss of her fading mind. Sometimes Lyana caught a glimpse of him in the corner of her eye and watched as he intently studied some aspect of the house. She found herself remembering the little boy she held in her arms, amazed at the years that had passed and how much he had grown. The structure of his face was changing from a little boy to a young man, looking more and more like his father every day.

Watching him made her wish she could just hold onto the moments. She knew the years would go quickly before both kids were out of the house. Would she still be around then? She shuddered at the thought.

• • •

The night when he learned about his mother's illness, after everyone had gone to bed, Zach was deep into a comprehensive study of bees when his eyes began to glaze over. He decided to take a break from staring at his computer and test one of his theories about the house.

He was apprehensive and cautious considering what had happened before, but he couldn't let this go until he knew for certain. He slowly walked to the intercom. He needed to know without a doubt. He leaned in closer and closed his eyes before he pressed the button.

Muted.

He quickly walked away and jumped into his bed, wrapping his blankets tightly around him. He lay there staring at the wall where he'd seen the symbol before the bees attacked, unable to fall asleep.

Wondering if it would work.

The next morning when Ariel came downstairs and couldn't speak *again,* he couldn't believe it. He tried to hide the look of excitement on his face.

Oh, my goodness, could it be!? His mind was racing. Still, it wasn't enough.

He decided to test his theory further, to confirm it.

Ariel took the brunt of his experiments, with no knowledge of what he was doing. He knew his dad had a full plate trying to accept all that was happening, and he certainly wasn't going to confirm his suspicions using his mother—she was already struggling. He secretly got a lot of pleasure out of his experiments; each time Ariel came down the steps for breakfast in the morning. This went on for weeks.

What started with losing her voice progressed to other things.

One night, he switched their intercom channels. The next morning, she came downstairs counting everything. Everyone thought she was playing a joke, but he knew better.

He didn't stop there. With every confirmation, he wanted to take it a step further. The more he immersed himself in his quest, the more his previous desire to uncover the meaning of the symbol took a backseat to this new inexplicable discovery.

He sat at breakfast one morning, thinking about what he had done the night before, smirking as he ate his toast, just waiting for his sister to come down the steps. When she finally did, he sat up and inched toward the edge of his chair, leaning ever so slightly forward to see if it had worked.

"Did you guys hear that last night," Ariel asked.

Ian was at the coffee maker, brewing coffee. He turned when he heard Ariel.

"Hear what?"

Zach remained silent.

"That music."

"What music?"

"You know, that song you and Mom always sing to us."

Ian just kept looking at her with a blank stare.

"Um, the one with the big drum fill!"

Zach was on the verge of bursting out of his seat.

With a breath of frustration, she began singing the opening line to "In the Air Tonight."

"I figured you and Mom were playing it to help keep the memory alive?"

They had been playing meaningful songs for the last several weeks, using music to try to help Lyana make connections to her memories. It was Dr. Rapha's idea.

"It wasn't us. Zach?"

Zach got up from his seat, called out, "Wasn't me," and headed to the pantry to put away the loaf of bread he had grabbed earlier, and also to hide his excitement. Once out of sight, he laughed quietly to himself.

The night before, standing at the intercom, he had pushed the radio button and whispered, "Play our song." It was a request he was almost certain wouldn't work. He had figured out that by pushing certain buttons, he could mute his sister or confuse her, but this was the first time he had instructed the device to play a song that only their family would know held special meaning.

And the device had done just that! At least for Ariel.

He was twirling in circles, doing a victory dance in the pantry when he was interrupted.

"What are you doing in here?" Ian said with a smile and chuckle, having caught the tail end of the celebratory dance.

"Just having a little fun." He brushed it off but decided he had enough evidence now. He needed to tell someone about what he had figured out. "Can we talk soon?"

"Absolutely. Let me finish my coffee and get through the paper."

"Cool." Zach walked away nonchalantly, still barely containing his excitement.

As he passed Ariel, she looked at him with accusing eyes, but he just shrugged, then ran up to his room.

"… 13, 14, 15."

THIRTY-TWO

ONCE THE COFFEE was done brewing, with the morning paper tucked under his arm, Ian grabbed the two cups and met Lyana in the living room. They had moved the furniture around to make a seating area in front of the picture window looking out onto the front lawn. Between the colder temps and Lyana's weakened body, Ian wanted her to have a spot where she felt comfortable and could enjoy the sunlight. He was doing everything he could, all the while knowing there was nothing he could *really* do.

"Did you hear any of that?" he said with a smile as he handed her a mug.

"Hear what, love?" She had been gazing out the window and slowly turned her head toward him.

"Ariel fell asleep hearing our song last night."

Lyana's expression was a question mark at first, then she smiled sheepishly when it came to her.

"In The Air?"

Ian smiled back at her. "You remember."

He sat, then opened the paper with a snap. For a moment, he imagined someone glancing in their window to see what must look like the perfect Norman Rockwell couple, her sipping her coffee, him buried in a newspaper, both of them framed by light coming in the big picture window. All that was missing from that picture was a pipe held in his right hand.

If only they knew …

"Ian, I'm scared."

The Norman Rockwell painting melted back into reality. He was scared too, and as much as he wanted to crumble and admit that to her, he knew he needed to stay strong. He needed to carry the hope she was quickly losing to this horrific disease. He had watched her go from shocked and angry, to sad and hopeless all within the span of a few weeks. The last thing she needed was for him to lose hope as well.

"We will get through this," he assured her. He wanted to believe that, he really did.

On most days while she would rest, he would go to his study and sob. Between his reading and using the room as a safe place to break down, he spent untold hours there. When he wasn't tucked away in his study, he was helping the kids with their homework, or trying to find the emotional energy to invite them to play a game or work on a puzzle together or do something, anything that might take their minds off the harsh truth about their mother's deteriorating condition.

"I'm done." Lyana had finished her coffee and set the mug on the table between them. "Can you help me to the couch?" Ian put down his mug and paper and helped her out of the chair. He walked her over to the couch and got her settled before grabbing the mugs and putting them in the kitchen sink.

By the time he returned to the living room, Lyana was asleep. He grabbed his paper and was just about to go to his study when he paused. He looked outside the picture window. A patchy dusting of snow covered much of the lawn, reminding him what time of the year it was.

With everything that had happened over the last few months, time had slipped away. He could hardly believe it was nearly Christmas. Lyana had always been the one to get excited about Christmas each year, pulling the decorations out immediately after Thanksgiving and making sure the house was vibrant and bright for the festivities.

As Ian watched her sleeping peacefully, he got an idea and ran upstairs.

"Zach, come help me with this."

Ian grabbed the pull cord in the hallway that led to the attic. Zach appeared just in time to help his dad catch the unfolding stairs.

"What's going on?" Zach asked as he followed his dad up the stairs. Ian pulled at the swinging string in front of him, turning on the single bulb that lit the cavernous attic. The huge space was occupied only by seasonal decorations and scattered, unmarked boxes they had tossed up there while unpacking. Ian shuffled across the wood planks that served as a floor to gather up the boxes marked "Christmas."

"We're going to put up the Christmas stuff?!" Zach's excitement confirmed that this was a good idea after all.

"We can have that chat you were asking about while we decorate, if you like."

Zach and Ian made several trips up and down the attic stairs, pulling boxes of decorations out one at a time. Zach's curiosity had him wandering around the space, careful to stay on the rickety planks so as not to fall through the ceiling below. Ian noticed he was staring at the corner of the attic.

"Dad, check this out." He motioned for Ian to come over.

The exposed wiring looked like a complex highway interchange. It was an intriguing mess of wires, and definitely out of the ordinary.

Ian examined the wires.

"What do you think it means?" asked Zach. Ian thought that was a strange way to word the question, but he answered anyway.

"I don't know. The house is old, so maybe it's just the way it was wired. I mean, over the years, they probably had to rewire things once or twice. I suppose they just left the old ones in place when they did that."

Zach stepped closer and reached out his hand toward the wires.

"Don't touch that," Ian said, a little more strongly than he intended. "I mean, the wires probably aren't live, but it's better to be safe than sorry …"

"… or electrocuted," added Zach.

"Exactly." Ian noticed an open box of miscellaneous items near where Zach was standing. "Hey, Zach—see if you can find some electrical tape in there. I think that's where we left it …"

Sure enough, Zach fished around and found an almost new roll of tape.

"Here you go, Dad."

He handed Ian the tape.

"Why don't you take this last box downstairs while I use the tape to cover the exposed wires. Just in case, you know?" He handed Zach the box and began taping over the wires. "I'll call Marshall later to come take a look. He'll know what this … means."

Zach reluctantly picked up the box and took it back downstairs.

When Ian exited the attic and went downstairs, he saw Zach meticulously organizing and laying out decorations. He had just started on the large box of ornaments that was practically overflowing from years of collecting tree decorations from places they had visited or purchased for special moments.

"Dad, are we going to get a real tree or are we going to put up this old thing?" Zach was pointing to a box that had layers of duct tape holding it together. Every year they talked about getting a real tree, but more times than not, they simply put up the fake tree because it was easier.

"Let's put up this one. That way we can show your mom when she wakes up."

Zach and Ian quietly pieced together the artificial tree, positioning it right in front of the picture window. Ian had moved the table to make room for it. They were being as quiet as possible since Lyana was still asleep on the couch. They didn't want to wake her.

"Dad, can we talk now?"

There were lots of decorations yet to sort through, but the tree was up, so Ian nodded and led Zach to the kitchen so they wouldn't disrupt Lyana's rest.

Zach picked up a pencil that was on the table and fidgeted with it while he spoke. "Dad, I think there is something strange going on with this house."

Ian sat down across from Zach and nodded. "I know you've been thinking about this a lot. Tell me more."

Zach explained what he had been doing with the intercom and how he believed it was affecting Ariel. He talked about the connection between his prompts and the things that happened to her—her lost voice, hearing things, acting strangely.

Ian didn't say anything. He was already struggling to accept what was happening to Lyana; having to think about the oddities of the house on top of that was just too much. He agreed with Zach that there was something more going on at Farr Hill, but concluded that Zach's explanation linking what was happening to Lyana to the house was just a wild attempt to make sense of everything.

Ms. Lewis had warned Ian this might happen, that the kids might come up with far-fetched ideas about how to fix their mother or how they could make it all better. It was common in situations like theirs as family members grasp at anything they can find a glimmer of hope.

Zach continued, describing the symbol he had seen on the night of the hive attack, and that it was the same one at Marshall's shack. When he had returned from the hospital, he discovered the drawing of the symbol underneath his bed. It had likely drifted there in the commotion of everything that had happened.

"I've been researching the symbol. I don't know much yet, but I'm ninety-seven percent certain it's ancient." Ian acknowledged the excitement in Zach's voice as he described the symbol but wasn't ready to engage or encourage Zach. He had a fuzzy memory of a symbol as well, but it was just at the edges of his memory, so it quickly faded. He decided to deflect, instead.

"This is very interesting. But … you need to stop teasing your sister."

Zach's eyes went wide. He didn't see that coming. Deflated, he said, "Fine," then scooted away from the table. "I'll go get Ariel so we can hang the ornaments on the tree."

With his head lowered in defeat, he walked away.

Ian felt terrible for dismissing Zach's inventive claims, but his attention quickly shifted to his wife, who remained still and silent on the couch. She looked so peaceful. He decided to let her continue resting and hoped they would finish decorating the tree so when she woke up, they could look at all the ornaments together—a trip down memory lane. He was doing everything he could to help her hold on.

"Tree time!" Ariel said with a skip in her step. Ian put a finger to his lips and pointed to Lyana. "Oops, sorry," she whispered. "But I just love decorating the tree."

The three of them worked together, pulling ornaments from the box, sharing stories of past Christmases and other family memories, talking about where each ornament came from. Before they knew it, the box was empty, and the tree was full.

"Let's wait for Mom to do the star." Ariel insisted they couldn't put the finishing touch on the tree without her. Ian and Zach agreed.

"Okay. We can take a break until she wakes up," said Ian. The three of them went their separate ways and agreed that once she was awake, they would finish the tree.

Ian went to his study to check his email. After the night of the storm, he had taken photos of the house and property and sent them to a professor of archeology he had met at the conference in Germany earlier that year. He was curious about their new surroundings and had a hunch this professor might see something in the photos that he might have missed. He didn't quite know what he was expecting his colleague to find, but his gut told him there might be something. Likely not anything that would substantiate Zach's claims, but any information could shed light on the growing mysteries about the house.

He opened his computer and looked through his emails, but there was nothing. He took a deep breath and just as he let out a long exhale, he noticed the candelabra, tucked away amongst a pile of books in the corner of a shelf. It was in the same place it had been since the morning after the storm when he and Lyana were in his study talking about it.

Ian picked it up and surveyed it closely. It was the first time he had studied it in detail. He turned it from side to side noticing the exquisite details on the drip pan, arms, and column down to its tarnished base. He didn't know what he was looking for, if he was looking for anything at all. He was about to put it on top of another stack of books when he turned it over. A faded marking roughly etched onto the bottom caught his attention.

Where have I seen this? Before he could collect his thoughts and find an answer, he heard Ariel calling from the living room.

"Mom is awake."

Ian left the study and walked into the living room. Ariel was sitting next to Lyana on the couch. Zach arrived a moment later.

Right, the tree, thought Ian. How could he have forgotten about that?

Lyana was surrounded by her family and could surely see what they had done, but each time she opened her mouth to speak, no words came.

"Mom?" Ariel said. She turned to Lyana and pleaded with her eyes.

Lyana just sat there, frozen.

"Dad, what's wrong with her?" Zach's voice wavered.

"Ly, hon. We're here." Ian tried to coax her to come back to them, like he had done so many times before when she was having an episode. But this time she wasn't responding.

• • •

I can see you! I can hear you!

The words formed in her head, but no sound came out of her mouth. She couldn't move her hands. She couldn't move at all. Her mind was racing but her body was still. She felt trapped.

Oh no. It's happening. Not yet. I'm not ready.

• • •

"Mom!!" Zach cried out.

His mother's eyes were open, but she wasn't responding. She just sat there, unmoving. Distant and detached.

Ariel screamed, "Dad, call Dr. Rapha!"

Ian grabbed his cell phone and began dialing.

"Hello?" The voice on the other line picked up and Ian walked away explaining the situation to the doctor. When he disappeared around the corner with the phone up to his ear, there was a knock on the front door.

Ariel motioned for Zach to get the door. "I'll stay with Mom," she said.

Zach heard his dad's voice as he walked to the door. "She's just gone," he kept saying over and over.

Zach opened the door to find Marshall. He quickly pulled him by the arm into the living room, explaining in broken sentences that something was wrong.

• • •

Marshall looked around, taking in all that was happening. Ian was on the phone, pacing in the next room, Ariel was sitting next to her mother, and Zach was holding onto his arm for dear life.

"I was just coming over to check out the attic," he said. He was surprised to see fear on the kids' faces, and a blank stare on Lyana's.

"Can you help her?" Ariel asked.

She spoke with such familiarity, like he was part of the family. It took him by surprise.

He sat down next to Lyana. "Ian is calling for help, Lyana." Her expression didn't change.

• • •

Lyana felt the couch shift as someone sat next to her. As Marshall moved into view to speak, her heart beat faster as panic started rising.

Who is this man? Why is he in my house? How do the kids know him? Where is Ian? Somebody help me!

She needed to scream but nothing would come out.

• • •

Ian hung up the call and joined them in the living room. Ariel was pacing behind the couch. Marshall was sitting next to Lyana, but watching Zach, who was staring at the decorated tree, counting something out loud.

"What are you counting, Zach?" Ian asked.

He paused, said, "The ornaments," then went right back to it.

Ian decided to wait until he was done with his count before relaying what the doctor said, but Ariel clearly didn't want to wait.

"What did the doctor say?" she asked, her voice just on the edge of panic.

"Great, I lost count," said Zach. He started again.

"Hey bud, can you put the count on hold for a minute?" Ian said. "I want to tell you what the doctor said."

Zach nodded.

"Doctor Rapha said we're supposed to just settle down and talk with Mom like we normally would. And include her in everything we do, as if things were just fine."

"But they're not fine, Dad!" said Ariel.

"I know, I know honey. But he says this is the best way to help. Maybe some sense of normal can help." He pointed to one of the decorations. "Remember when we got this one?"

"That's from the Franklin Park Zoo," said Zach. He had abandoned his ornament count.

Ariel walked over to the tree and lifted an ornament that she had made a few years before in an art class. It was a glass star decorated with acrylic paints. The paint had peeled off one of the points on the star and as she held it up, the sun hit it, reflecting light directly onto Lyana and the necklace that was resting on her chest.

"What a beautiful piece," Marshall said as he removed his gloves and bent down to tie his boot.

• • •

Out of the corner of her eye, Lyana caught a glimpse of his hand and what appeared to be a tattoo. She could only see a small portion of it but as she studied it, her eyes widened. She had seen that tattoo before.

What is happening?

Marshall leaned over and whispered into her ear, *"At the end of the dark night, there IS light."* Then he stood up, the tattoo disappearing under the sleeve of his jacket.

• • •

"Kids, why don't you stay here with your mother and keep sharing stories about the ornaments?" I'm sure your mom would love that." Ian tilted his head to the side, motioning for Marshall to follow him. "I need Marshall to check something out for me."

The two went to the attic, where Ian showed Marshall the cluster of wires that was now hidden underneath black tape.

"Do you know anything about this?"

"May I?" Marshall gestured at the mess, then pulled the tape back to look at what was going on underneath. He studied the wires for a moment, but otherwise didn't move. "I don't think it's a problem," he said finally, then placed the tape back over the wires.

"Are you sure?"

"Mostly sure," said Marshall. "But I'd like to bring my tools and take a closer look, just in case."

They walked back downstairs. The kids were talking a mile a minute.

"Dad, it was like she was here," they both said in unison. Then they were shouting over one another.

"When we pointed to the star, she made a sound," said Zach.

"It was a gasp," corrected Ariel. "Like she'd been holding her breath."

"It didn't last long …"

"It was only a second …"

"But she was back. I know it …"

"And then she was gone again," added Ariel.

The two kids were finally silent.

"Okay, hang on, we'll talk about this in a minute." He ushered Marshall out the door and stepped outside with him into the cold.

"I'm sorry, Marshall. I don't know what to tell you. She's gotten worse, you know? And the kids …" Ian's voice caught.

"I understand, Ian. Look, you've got a lot on your plate tonight. I'll come back tomorrow to take a closer look at the wires in the attic. Meanwhile, if you need anything, don't hesitate to ask. Okay?"

Marshall looked Ian in the eye, then nodded and turned to go.

Ian shut the door and returned his attention to his family. He listened intently as Zach and Ariel explained in detail what they had witnessed.

Ian knew not to get his hopes up, but there was no denying that this was at least a glimmer of hope. They continued to share memories about the ornaments, then placed the star in her lap. Ian watched Lyana's face, looking for any sign of recognition. *Hoping*.

• • •

Ian's expression was so sad, it made Lyana want to cry.

She wanted so desperately to reach out and hug each of them. She was a prisoner trapped inside her own body, unable to move or speak, questioning if what was happening around her was real or some fiction of her untrustworthy mind. Thoughts and memories would arrive, then immediately slip away. She fought to remember what she'd just been recalling and failed. But she could see her family. Right there. Right in front of her.

"Be with me, Lyana," Ian said. His voice sounded so broken.

I'm trying, Ian! I'm trying so hard, but I can't find my way back!

• • •

As the minutes turned to hours, the glimmer of hope Ian had held onto slipped from his hands.

THIRTY-THREE

IAN WAS UP early. He had carried Lyana to bed the night before and brought her back downstairs and propped her up in her chair, hoping the sunlight might help. She hadn't spoken a word since the night before and in an instant, Ian went from husband to caretaker. He made breakfast for the kids, knowing all of this was difficult for both of them.

A stack of pancakes sat on the counter waiting for Zach. Next to the pancakes, a plate of avocado toast and eggs for Ariel. Ian's eyes were heavy and restless. He had barely slept and was already on his third cup of coffee when Marshall arrived.

• • •

The knock at the door woke Zach, who had stayed up late researching. He managed to find the contact information for one of the previous owners, who, according to the real estate records had only stayed at Farr Hill for eighteen months. He traced them to a coastal town in Maine and located a phone number for them.

He was planning to make that call while Ian and Marshall were distracted in the attic, but his plan was sidetracked when he saw the pancakes.

"It can wait until after breakfast," he whispered under his breath.

"Did you say something?" Ian asked as he and Marshall made their way to the attic.

"Yeah. Thanks for the pancakes!"

"You got it, kiddo," his dad called from the stairs. "Let your sister know when she wakes up that there is something special for her, too."

"Will do," he hollered back, pouring a layer of syrup on the stack of pancakes.

As he cut into them and began eating, he stared intently at the puzzle he and Ariel had put together. It had taken them so long. It was like an optical illusion that if you stared at it long enough, something else might appear.

• • •

In the attic, Marshall and Ian were discussing the history of the house. Ian was still curious about the man who built it and was asking Marshall questions about his uncle to uncover anything that might help.

"What can you tell me about him?"

Marshall was vague and seemed uncomfortable as he discussed Mr. Goodpasture, explaining to Ian that he hadn't spent a lot of time with him over the years. He had grown up hearing stories about the house and knew he collected antiques and said there was likely a lot of history at Farr Hill. But that was the extent of what Marshall was willing to offer and he quickly turned his attention to the wires.

"Let's get to work." Marshall slowly pulled back the tape that was draped over the wires just like he had the night before to get a closer look.

• • •

Zach had devoured half the stack of pancakes when he heard his mother gasp for air in the next room. He ran to her. By the time he got there, she was unresponsive. *Did I really hear her?* Confused, he went back to the kitchen to finish his breakfast.

• • •

Marshall placed the tape back over the wires and explained to Ian that they should be covered, just to be safe.

"We can use an electrical box," he said. "I'm pretty sure there's a spare in the tool shed out back."

After everything else that had already happened at the house, the last thing Ian wanted to think about was a house fire. He agreed it was a good plan.

"I don't know much about electrical stuff, but I'm willing to help," said Ian. "I'll just follow your lead."

"It shouldn't be too difficult." He stood and walked over to the stairs. "I'll be right back."

•••

Zach looked up from his plate of pancakes to see Marshall exit through the front door. He was back within a few minutes, carrying a metal junction box, then headed upstairs.

Moments later, he heard it again, his mother gasping in the next room. He dropped his fork and ran to her.

For the first time in a day, there was life in her eyes. Her mouth was moving like she was trying to say something. Zach leaned in closer.

"Azar," she whispered as she held his arm.

He felt her hands loosen their grip and watched as her eyes faded back into the darkness. As quickly as she had shown signs of consciousness, she was gone.

"Mom! Mom?" He was begging her to come back, if even for a moment. "What were you trying to say?" he pleaded. He took a deep breath, then lowered his voice. "Be with us ..." he began.

"Breakfast looks amazing." Ariel's voice startled Zach. He turned to see her standing near the kitchen. He tried to explain to her that their mother had been *awake* for a moment, but he could tell she didn't want to engage in the conversation. Instead, he followed her to the kitchen to finish his breakfast.

He sat silently, looking at the few bites left on his plate, poking them with his fork while Ariel talked about how excited she was to go back to school after the first of the year. He was frustrated. He was certain he had heard his mother earlier and this second instance just confirmed that. *But how?* He was unwilling to accept that what happened was simply part of her diagnosis.

He stared at the puzzle, searching for answers. He picked up the box. *Bgraamiens Flowing Rainbow Lines Puzzle. 1,000 pieces.* He didn't know what he was looking for, he just wanted to find something, anything. Empty-handed, he went back to the pancakes.

As he took the last bite, it came to him.

"That's it!" He dropped his fork onto the plate of sticky syrup. "See all the colored threads and how they are woven through each other?"

He started comparing the lines in the puzzle to the loose wires. Ariel looked at him, a confused expression on her face.

He leaped out of his chair and ran up the stairs, yelling, "Stop!" When he made it to the attic, he shouted it again. "Stop!"

Ian and Marshall stopped what they were doing and turned to Zach in unison.

"Whoa, slow down, Zach," Ian said.

"It's the wires," Zach said, trying to catch his breath between the words. "When you were doing something with the wires, Mom came back!"

Marshall and Ian exchanged a look.

"What do you mean she came back?" asked Ian. "She's back?" He stood suddenly, as if ready to sprint back down the rickety attic stairs to see for himself.

"No, no. She's not back now. But ..." Zach paused to order the words in his head. "When you were working on the wires, I heard Mom gasp," he said. "I'm sure of it."

"How sure?" asked Marshall.

"Um … pretty sure?"

Ian sat back down. "I don't know, Zach. That seems a bit like a coincidence, don't you think?"

The answer was right there, but Zach couldn't quite see it, like he was staring at it through a thick patch of fog. Still, he knew he was onto something. He started again. "It's the wires …"

"Zach, I get it. You want Mom to be okay. We all do. But why do you think the wires have anything to do with this? You weren't up here with …"

"Can we just try something? Please?"

The intercom. The lamp-post. The wires in the attic. Was everything connected back to the house? They have to believe me. They have to try!

"Dad, please!" Zach was nearly in tears.

Marshall was nearly done covering the wires, only the last two screws remained to fully fasten the box in place. He stopped what he was doing and looked not to Ian for direction, but to Zach. Tears began to form in Zach's eyes. He brushed them away with the back of his hand.

"I … okay," Ian said, "We can try."

Zach knew that look. His dad didn't believe him. But at least he was willing to try.

"What do you want us to do?" Ian asked.

"I'll stay here with Marshall," Zach began, his disappointment suddenly replaced with excitement. "You go down to be with Mom, okay? Yell when you get there. And then we'll try something with the wires?" He looked to Marshall, who nodded.

A couple minutes later Zach heard his father say, "I'm here."

At Zach's instruction, Marshall slowly removed the box that was covering the wires. He held it apart from the wires for a few seconds, then started to put it back when Zach grabbed his wrist. Marshall turned around suddenly. There was a strange look in the caretaker's eyes—like he was searching for something. Zach shrugged it off.

"Wait just a minute more," he said.

• • •

Ian sat next to Lyana when he came down to the living room, only to see that she didn't look any different than before. When he called up to Zach and Marshall to say that he was here, he took Lyana's hand and turned his attention to the front window. He didn't want to be looking at her when Zach's wild theory inevitably failed. That would be hard to take, even though he knew it was unlikely to begin with.

And then he felt it.

Lyana's grip tightened. He turned back to her.

She gasped. And then her eyes came alive.

"Ian," she said, her voice a raspy whisper.

He couldn't believe it. Ian hugged her, "I'm here," he said. "And so are …" But before he could finish the sentence, she was gone again.

Ian waited a moment more, silently urging her to return. She remained a blank page. Ian let go of her hand and raced back up the stairs to the attic.

The box had been placed back over the wires. Marshall was fastening the screws, affixing them to the beam.

"Wait!" Ian was leaning over to catch his breath. "I think Zach is right. What did you do?"

"We uncovered the wires," said Zach. "But then Marshall covered them again." Zach shot Marshall a smirk and grabbed the screwdriver from his hand and began unfastening the screws. "I told you so." The plastic box fell to the floor and as it did, they could hear Ariel yelling from downstairs.

"She's back!"

They all rushed downstairs.

Lyana was indeed back. Her body was weak, and she was whispering incoherently under her breath, but she was there. The three of them gathered around her. Ian reached out for her hand. She gripped his hand back, then smiled a crooked smile, first at Zach, then at Ariel.

• • •

"Wait, I have an idea," said Zach. He left his mother's side and raced over to Marshall, who was coming down the stairs. "We need to go back up," he said. Marshall hesitated, but then Ian joined them and led the way.

"Stay with Mom," Zach called out to Ariel.

"I'm not going anywhere," she called back.

The three of them crouched near the wall where the wires remained exposed.

"Where do these wires lead?" Zach asked, studying them closely. When he'd had his moment of clarity earlier, he was thinking about how much the puzzle they'd been working on reminded him of a picture of brain wiring. He'd seen something like that in one of his schoolbooks. The wires in the attic looked eerily similar.

Marshall and Ian exchanged another look. Zach continued with his pleas for them to explore further, but this time they didn't hesitate. Marshall pulled back one of the wall panels that covered where the wires seemed to lead.

There were at least fifty different wires of several different colors crossing over one another, covered in dust and cobwebs. When Marshall had pulled back the board, a distinct smell wafted out of the space. It smelled like a mixture of melting plastic and cat urine. Zach nearly vomited at the intense smell and had to leave the attic for a minute.

Marshall came down the attic stairs a moment later wearing a dust mask. He handed one to Zach.

"Where'd you get those?" Zach asked, his fingers still pinching his nose.

"I always keep a few around," he said. "Never leave home without 'em." He offered a slight smile.

"What *was* that smell?" Zach asked. He stopped pinching his nose long enough to put the mask on.

"When wires are left exposed, they can fray and sometimes the connection points melt. There's a chemical reaction that takes place and …" He paused. "That's what makes the smell."

"It smells awful."

"That smell is a warning. Wires in this condition can be quite dangerous. Last night I thought it was nothing, but now … I'm not so sure."

"So now what do we do?" asked Zach.

Ian came up the attic stairs. He was also wearing a mask. "I think we need to find the main electric panel. Am I right?" He looked over at Marshall.

"Indeed, you are."

Ian started walking down the stairs. Zach followed behind, counting down from fifteen. His dad stopped on seven and Zach nearly bumped into him.

"Um …" He looked over his shoulder at Marshall. "Just where is the panel? I know I should probably know this, but …"

Marshall grabbed his tool bag and walked past them down the stairs. "Follow me," he said. Then he stopped, too—on step number three. He turned and pointed up to the bedrooms. "I meant to ask—you have any problems with the intercoms?"

"Actually, now that you mention it …" began Zach.

His dad finished his sentence for him. "… we've had a few problems." He looked directly at Zach as he added, "But nothing too out of the ordinary."

Marshall stood there, listening, then turned around and marched back up the stairs to Zach's room. He used his tools to remove the intercom box from the wall. Behind the box, the wires were another tangled mess.

"Wow," said Zach. "It's just like in the attic."

Marshall pulled down his mask and leaned in closer to smell the back of the electrical panel. His face said it all. He quickly pulled his mask up.

"You two go ahead. I'm going to secure the intercom back to the wall. I'll meet you at the breaker panel."

"Um … about that …" began Ian.

Marshall didn't look up as he pointed behind him at the stairs. "It's in the pantry."

Zach and Ian went downstairs, pausing to check on Lyana.

"How is she doing?" Ian asked Ariel.

"Quiet, but she's still here," she said.

Zach looked at his mom. Her eyes were alive and alert. And he was pretty sure she smiled, even if just a little.

"Let me know if anything changes. We're going to the pantry," said Ian. He gave Ariel a side hug, then he and Zach continued to the kitchen.

Marshall arrived a couple minutes later, squeezed past Ian and Zach, and removed the old mirror from the wall, leaning it up against the cabinets. The breaker panel was attached to the wall directly behind where the mirror once hung.

Zach held his breath as Marshall opened the panel.

"What on earth?!" exclaimed Ian.

"Whoa!" added Zach.

Wires were everywhere. Red, yellow, white, blue. The box that held them together was charred ever so slightly and emitted that distinct chemical smell.

"Is that smoke?" Ian asked, pointing.

"Rip it out!" Zach shouted. He knew his mom had worked hard on that pantry, but this was a life and death situation. *Or at least a pretty serious one*, thought Zach.

"Go ahead," Ian said.

Zach looked up at his father and saw a hint of excitement on his face.

Marshall left the pantry and returned moments later with a sledgehammer and crowbar.

"Might want to back up," he said.

He leaned the bar against the cabinet next to the mirror and positioned himself with the hammer, gripping it with both hands. Zach held his breath and reached for his father's hand.

The head of the sledgehammer met the wall, creating a gaping hole to the side of the breaker panel. The pantry filled with dust and debris.

Lyana let out a savage scream from the living room. There were no words, just an anguish-fueled, blood-curdling sound that echoed through the entire house.

Ian and Zach ran out of the kitchen into the living room. Ariel met them halfway and they ran back to Lyana, who was wailing in pain.

"We have to stop!" Zach said. "It's hurting her!"

Ian shook his head.

"I don't think so, Zach. I think … I think it's helping her."

"But …"

"Those wires … they're connected somehow. You were right, Zach. You were absolutely right. We have to fix it!" Ian turned to Ariel. "Stay with her," he said. Then he ran back to the pantry, Zach following close behind. Marshall was standing in the pantry, the sledgehammer still in his hands. The dust had settled, and they could see just a hint of what lay behind the electrical box.

"That's …" began Ian. He grabbed the crowbar and started prying away the plasterboard, widening the hole. With each press of the crowbar, Lyana let out another scream.

THIRTY-FOUR

T HE SICKLY BITTER smell permeated the entire pantry, seeping into the kitchen.

Zach found an old pair of gloves in Marshall's bag and started pulling jagged pieces of plaster from the wall between sledgehammer swings from Marshall and crowbar prying from his dad. Each time they stopped hammering at the wall, Lyana's screams faded away.

He felt like crying. It was so hard to hear his mother's cries. But Zach was the one who had figured it out. He was the one who made the connection between the house and his mother's episodes. And his dad was right—they had to get to the bottom of this.

When the last of the dust settled, his dad shined a flashlight in the open space. It was like nothing Zach had ever seen. The crossing of wires and frayed lines ran up the entire wall, some of them wrapped around another metal box. It looked like a massive tangle of rainbow spaghetti; a wild road map leading to nowhere. It looked like ... the puzzle Zach and Ariel had put together.

Zach reached in and grabbed the frayed ends of two old wires. He carefully rubbed them together. As he did, he could hear his mother screaming again from the other room.

"We need to fix this," said Ian.

"But how?" asked Zach. He couldn't imagine how they could sort through this mess.

"We need to rewire the entire house," said Marshall.

"Can we do that?" asked Ian. "Should we call an electrician? Did you know any of this was here? I thought you'd know everything about the house ..."

Marshall turned to look Ian directly in the eye, a hardened look on his face. "So did I." Then his expression softened. "I can do this," he said. "It will take some time, a week, maybe more, but I can do this."

"Do it!" said Zach and his dad at the same time.

"We'll need the blueprints for the house," said Marshall. He lugged the sledgehammer out of the pantry and rested it against the kitchen counter. Ian followed and set the crowbar on the floor next to it.

"I'm not sure where ..." began Ian.

"There's a box in the attic," offered Marshall. "In the far corner across from the electrical box. Blueprints should be in there."

• • •

Ian wasn't sure how he'd missed the box when they were moving in and carting stuff up to be stored in the attic, but sure enough, there it was: a dust-coated box labeled, *Akolo*.

I wonder what that means.

Ian made a mental note to ask about the strange word, then began digging through the box until he found the

228

blueprints. He brought them to the kitchen table where he and Marshall spread them out.

Marshall grabbed a pencil and began to sketch out a plan to update the electrical system. He talked as he worked, explaining to Ian how they could salvage certain elements of the existing system, and how they would radically transform the way everything connected at the main power box.

"I don't think we'll have to tear up any floors or ceilings for this. The wiring that needs to be replaced appears to be primarily in the walls."

Ian didn't know how he could be so sure. The mess of wires behind the pantry looked worse than the box of Christmas tree lights they had dumped on the living room floor.

"You are all really lucky," said Marshall.

"How so?" Ian looked at him curiously.

Before Marshall could answer, Zach called for his dad. He and Marshall went to the living room.

Zach and Ariel were sitting on either side of Lyana on the couch. She had stopped screaming but appeared to be going in and out of consciousness. With every wire that was touched or pulled from the panel, she would have a physical reaction—a jolt of energy to her body or a whimper in pain.

"Dad, it's like Mom is somehow connected to the wires, like she's part of the house," said Zach. "I know you didn't want to believe me but …"

"I believe you, Zach. I don't understand how or why, but you're right." He paused. "But we have a problem." He turned to Marshall. "We need to shut off the power so you can fix the wiring, but I'm afraid of what that might do to

Lyana. What if that hurts her … what if that …" he didn't want to say it.

Ariel didn't hesitate. "What if that kills her?!"

"Dad! I know what we can do!" Zach jumped up from the couch and walked to the front window. He pointed. "The lamp-post!"

"What do you mean, 'the lamp-post'?" asked Ian.

Zach turned to Marshall. "Where does the lamp-post get its power? During the storm, it stayed on when the power went off in the house. There must be a different source of electricity for the lamp-post!"

"He's right!" said Ariel. "I saw it myself."

"That is a mystery," said Marshall. "But I think I know where you're going with this. Don't touch any more wires. I'll be back shortly."

Ian watched him walk out the door, then turned to look at Lyana again. She looked haggard, exhausted. But she was alert, too. There was life in her eyes.

He hoped and prayed they were doing the right thing. This whole situation made absolutely no sense. But Zach had been right so far.

Maybe he would be right again.

• • •

Marshall ran back to the storage shed to grab jumper cables and some old electrical wire. Carrying the wire and cables in his arms, he sprinted around the side of the house to the lamp-post in the front yard and began digging. He glanced up at the picture window and saw Zach watching him, glued to the window like a child watching for Santa on Christmas Eve.

Marshall's shovel reached the metal box he was counting on finding with a loud "clang." He bent down and pried it open, revealing the wires that connected the post to its source of electricity. He then connected the braided wire from the spool to the negative and positive clamps on one end of the jumper cable, leaving the other end unattached near the junction box he'd uncovered. He slowly unwound the spool as he walked toward the house and in through the front door. He continued through the kitchen and into the pantry. There, he opened the second electrical box that they'd found and used a voltage detector to confirm what he believed was true: that it wasn't currently active. The voltage read "zero." He carefully connected the wire from the spool to the main positive and negative posts, then called Zach and Ian into the kitchen.

"Ian, I'm going to need you to turn off the power to the house when I say so." He showed Ian how at the electrical box with all the mixed-up wiring. "As soon as you do that, I'll connect the wires to the second box using the jumper cables out by the lamp-post. It'll take a couple seconds to hook those up, so the lights may be out for a short time."

"But what if that hurts Mom ..." said Zach.

"Zach, I'm going to be honest with you. I don't know if this is going to work. I'm ... I'm not entirely sure what this other electrical box is wired to—but if I'm right, we'll have power once it's connected to the lamp-post line. I'm going to need your help, though. I'll let you know when I've hooked up the jumper cables, but I need you to be my ears and eyes on your mother. Once I reconnect the power, I want you to watch her closely. If anything changes, run back to the door and tell me. Shout it loud, Zach."

Zach nodded and walked back to the living room. Marshall looked over at Ian. "If the power doesn't come on after I hook up the cables, flip the main power back on."

"But then how would you rewire the house?"

"Then we'll figure something else out. But I'm hoping we won't have to."

"Okay."

Marshall put his hand on Ian's shoulder. "It's going to work."

Marshall walked out to the lamp-post. The wind had picked up. It was a biting wind, the kind that found its way through every nook and cranny in your clothing. He crouched down at the cables, picked up the clamps.

"Now!" he shouted.

• • •

The lights went out. Zach started counting.

"1, 2, 3, 4, 5, 6 …"

When he reached "7," the lights flickered on for a second, then off again. Zach couldn't see his mother's condition. He'd forgotten his flashlight. And now he'd lost track of his count. Zach started to panic. A couple seconds later, the lights came back on. This time, they stayed on.

Lyana let out a long sigh, then closed her eyes. Her entire body relaxed.

Zach ran to the front door and yelled out at Marshall, "It worked! It worked!"

Ian joined Zach as they ran into the living room. Ariel had wrapped herself around her mother and was crying with relief. Zach joined her, wrapping his arms around them both.

"Zach, Ariel …" Ian's voice was gentle. "Your mom is going to need some rest now. This has been a traumatic experience for her."

Zach felt his dad's hand on his shoulder. Reluctantly, he pried himself away from his mother. Ariel had done the same.

"And besides," his dad continued. "It's my turn for a hug."

Zach smiled as his dad sat next to his mom and wrapped his arms around her. He kissed the top of her head and she leaned ever so slightly against him.

"You should carry her up to bed," said Ariel.

"Yeah," agreed Zach.

"You have very wise children, Ian." Marshall had slipped in during their happy reunion with Lyana. Zach observed that his nose and ears were red from the cold.

"Thank you, Marshall," said Ian. "I'm usually not short on words, but just … thank you."

"I'll put something over the wires out front to protect them from the elements, then I'll be on my way. I'll be back tomorrow to start work on the rewiring." He left through the front door, closing it gently behind him.

Ian gently lifted Lyana in his arms and carried her up the stairs. Zach was watching each step, willing his father to be careful and counting each one.

"… 13, 14, 15." Zach sighed with relief.

"You hungry?" Ariel asked.

"Yeah. We forgot to eat dinner," said Zach. "When have we ever forgotten to eat dinner?"

Ariel offered to make something and walked into the kitchen. Zach followed, careful to step around the boxes and bins that had been moved out of the pantry. It didn't smell quite so bad there now.

"Don't start yet, Ariel," said Zach. Before she could respond he had run out of the kitchen. He pushed open the front door and ran out into the cold. Marshall had collected all his tools and was walking away from the lamp-post.

"Marshall!" Zach called out. "Are you hungry?"

• • •

Ian carried Lyana upstairs and laid her in their bed. Her body went limp as soon as she was comfortably underneath the sheets. He rubbed her head and brushed back her silky dark hair.

"I don't know what's happening, but I will not let it end like this. I'm fighting for you, Ly," he whispered in her ear as a tear fell down his cheek. She fell asleep within minutes. Ian watched her chest rise and fall. She looked so peaceful. He turned off the light on the nightstand and quietly closed the door behind him.

Marshall was sitting at the kitchen table with the kids when he came downstairs.

"Saved you a place," said Zach.

Ariel had made her signature dish: grilled cheese sandwiches and tomato soup. Ian couldn't think of a more perfect meal.

After a few bites, Ian looked up at Marshall. "What did you mean earlier? We are lucky?" He sure didn't feel lucky as he looked around at the mess that was once his kitchen, the pantry destroyed with wires everywhere, his wife upstairs battling a disease he couldn't wrap his head around.

"It could have been a lot worse," Marshall answered. "I did a little research when I got my gear for the power switchover. Turns out that smell coming from the attic and behind the walls was a result of a chemical reaction between the old, tinned copper wiring and newer aluminum wiring. When those two elements combine under the right conditions, gaseous hydrogen is released."

"Is that bad?" asked Ariel.

"Not only could there have been a fire, but that gas can cause intense hallucinations."

"Really?" said Zach.

"That's crazy," said Ariel.

Ian just nodded. It was all starting to make sense.

• • •

Later that night, Zach lay awake in his bed. Something was still bugging him. While the gas thing might explain the strange things his mom—really, all of them—were seeing, it still didn't explain the beehive in his wall or the way he could use the intercom to affect his sister. There was no way that could be explained away as mere coincidence.

There is definitely more to this.

THIRTY-FIVE

MARSHALL ARRIVED AT the crack of dawn to start work on the rewiring. Ian had heard him come through the front door. He climbed out of bed, careful not to trouble Lyana's sleep, and went downstairs to brew some coffee.

Zach and Ariel showed up in the kitchen a few minutes later. They grabbed a box of cereal each and went to the living room to eat straight from the box and watch the recap of *American Idol* from the night before.

"Is there anything I can do to help?" Ian asked Marshall.

He didn't turn around, still focused on his work in the pantry. "Not at the moment," he said. "It's going surprisingly well."

"Well, there's coffee if you want it," Ian said. Then he went upstairs to check on Lyana. When he opened the door to their bedroom, he was stunned at what he saw. She was sitting up in their bed. The life was back in her eyes.

"Are you back?" He didn't even know what to say as he slowly approached her. She smiled at him. It was the first time he had seen her smile in what seemed like forever. He sat on the side of the bed next to her and hugged her.

"I'm back," she said calmly.

"But how?" He couldn't believe it.

She was tired and her body weak, but her mind was sharp.

"Ian, before you get the kids, I need to tell you something."

Ian braced himself for the possibility of bad news.

She continued. "I heard my mother's voice. As I lay on the couch paralyzed, I saw her standing next to the Christmas tree that the kids were decorating. It was the strangest thing."

This wasn't at all what Ian had expected. He reached up and brushed a stray stand of hair from Lyana's face and nodded, encouraging her to continue.

"Ian, in that moment, I finally understood her. She had become so emotionally and physically paralyzed from her own abusive relationship with Stan, she didn't know *how* to protect us. She *couldn't* protect us." She took a deep breath. "She came and stood next to me and whispered 'I have always loved you.' It felt so real."

There was something different about her. Ian could see the change in her eyes. Lyana knew it was just a vision, but the experience had a noticeable effect on her.

"I can finally let go of the hurt I have been carrying for so long." She pulled Ian closer in a hug. "I can finally forgive her."

They held each other in silence for a long time. Ian was so happy to have his Lyana back.

Lyana looked up at Ian as tears rolled down her cheek. "Now, go get the kids," she said.

Ian called down for Zach and Ariel to join them upstairs.

"Mom?" Ariel let out a squeal of excitement. Zach couldn't even put together words. They both ran to her and hugged her.

After a moment, Ian gently touched the kids on their shoulders. "We should probably give her some space." Ian was concerned too much commotion might cause her to become restless, or worse, lost again.

The kids sat at the foot of the bed. Lyana shifted her position so she could look right at them.

"Thank you for putting up the Christmas tree. That was such a brilliant idea and it meant so much to me. It was so frustrating for me, you know? I could see and hear you, but I couldn't respond, and I so desperately wanted to. And the stories you told about all the ornaments? Those were so great."

Before they knew it, an hour had passed. Ian didn't want to question the gift of this time with Lyana, knowing she could be gone at any time. He wanted to revel it in.

He walked to the bedroom window and pulled back the curtains.

"Look at this!" He motioned for the kids to join him. They all stared in amazement.

The fog had lifted. The fog that seemed to perpetually surround Farr Hill was gone and they could clearly see the sun poking out through the trees. Ian helped Lyana off the bed, then wrapped his arm around her and walked with her to the window. The smile on her face was radiant. He lifted her off her feet and twirled her around. It felt like a miracle.

"Way to give Mom space, Dad," Ariel snarked, but there was a smile on her face. The four of them laughed, filling the house with a sound it hadn't heard in far too long.

• • •

Marshall continued working on the rewiring, and as he did, Lyana gained more and more strength. Her mind was beginning to catch up with her body. She was coming back to life.

They had all watched it happen right in front of their eyes, including Marshall. Lyana knew that if her family members had been the only ones to see it, they might have questioned it. But knowing Marshall was witnessing the same thing solidified that it was true. She was improving. As the house was being fixed, wire by wire, piece by piece, so was she.

"Mom, we saved the star for you."

Lyana was smiling from ear to ear and asked Ian to grab a chair from the kitchen. He placed it near the tree, and steadied her as she climbed on top, leaning into the tree on her tiptoes before placing the star on the tree.

"There we go!" she exclaimed. "Now it's ready."

Joy filled the living room for the first time in months. The sun was shining in through the picture window and there was a lightness in the air after months of heaviness and uncertainty.

Lyana noticed Marshall walking to the front door with his bag of tools. She called him over. He set the tool bag down and joined them in the living room.

"That's a lovely tree," he said. He examined a few of the ornaments. "And full of history, I see."

"Yeah, lots of memories in that tree," said Lyana.

"And many more to come," said Marshall.

Lyana walked over and gave him a hug. In that moment, she didn't care if he was a hugger or not. She was just so grateful for all he had done for her, for their family. The two had become fast friends as they regularly enjoyed morning chats over coffee while the rest of the family slept. She was comfortable around him, there was an unexpected warmth to him. Though he was a man of few words, he was easy to talk to. He was patient when she struggled to recall something or paused to search for the right words.

There were more than a few moments that remained a blur or were simply gone, including one specific moment while she was still lost while sitting in front of the Christmas tree. She sensed that this moment was important. That it meant something. But it remained just out of reach. So many things had wandered into the periphery of her brain yet couldn't find their way back. She didn't fear disappointing Marshall if she didn't recall something important. He had become a sounding board and a trusted friend. In a way, he had become family.

Marshall accepted the hug without a hint of resistance. Lyana thought she even saw the remnant of a tear in his eyes when she stepped back.

Marshall cleared his throat. "There's still some cosmetic work to do," he said. "But the re-wiring is complete. Everything has been switched over. The old wires are no more."

Lyana hadn't even noticed him do that. But sure enough, the braided wire that had run across the floor from the front door to the pantry was gone. She glanced out at the lamp-post. The hole he'd dug a week earlier had already been filled.

"I'll come back later in the week to finish the drywall repairs," he said.

Ian walked over to him and shook his hand. "You don't know how much this means to us."

He smiled and nodded over at the kids, who were beaming. "Oh, I think I have an idea." Then he winked, zipped up his jacket, slung his tool bag over his shoulder, and walked through the front door.

Ian shut the door behind him, then he and Lyana walked arm in arm to the picture window. The kids joined them there and they all watched as Marshall walked away. He turned one last time to nod farewell, then disappeared around the corner.

"It's going to be okay," she said. "Everything is going to be okay. We're home."

THIRTY-SIX

THE SNOW HAD all but melted and signs of spring were everywhere. It had been a few months since Lyana's miraculous recovery and while there were still scattered moments of confusion, exhaustion, and lost memories, for the most part she was back to herself. The kids had returned to school. Ian was thriving in his work, preparing for another overseas conference. Lyana had even helped Marshall with the final cosmetic repairs around the house and was writing music again.

The news of Lyana's recovery had spread like wildfire through the medical community. Dr. Rapha had spent months trying to learn more in hopes of discovering a medical breakthrough that could save other families from similar situations. He had also started speaking across the country at seminars, discussing the connection between dangerous chemicals in older homes and the brain, and how being exposed to the gases could result in symptoms that presented as dementia. His findings and lectures were already being implemented in teaching hospitals across the country. Further research on the matter has also led to rewritten building codes in several states.

The Keanes knew and understood there was much more to her recovery than medical miracles. Marshall was the only other person who knew the full extent of what they had experienced at Farr Hill, and while he would often dismiss it as coincidence or point it back to the faulty wiring, he knew the house *was* special. Goodpasture had made sure of that.

"Could you imagine if we told anyone about all of this?" Lyana said one lazy afternoon.

"I've thought about that a lot," said Ian.

They had agreed to keep most of what they experienced to themselves. They were convinced that if anyone heard the truth, they wouldn't believe it. They just didn't want to open themselves up to that type of scrutiny. The kids were instructed to do the same. They had found a reasonable, if unlikely, connection between the old house and Lyana's brain, but there were still moments that simply couldn't be explained. How did brain-altering chemicals account for the direct, immediate pain she felt when Marshall and Ian were tearing apart the pantry wall?

Lyana was convinced it had something to do with the reason she felt so drawn to the house in the first place, from the moment she stumbled across the listing to the minute they arrived. The fact that her family was the closest they had ever been after everything they had endured only further confirmed for her that this was where they were always meant to be. Despite everything that happened, or maybe because of it, she believed that being there represented something more. There was strange comfort for her in that.

Lyana had already placed two mugs neatly on the countertop waiting for the coffee to finish brewing. Marshall had also recently introduced her to karkade tea. He brought it over for her one morning as a gift and it had since become her morning drink of choice.

Ian was propped up on a stool at the kitchen island with his paper. Lyana poured his coffee, handed it to him, and prepped her tea before pulling a stool out for herself.

"There is something I keep coming back to." She brought the mug to her lips and blew on it ever so slightly, still too hot to drink.

Ian lowered the paper, looking at her curiously over the top of the glasses that sat on the tip of his nose. "What's that?"

"What if it *was* something more?"

Ian's eyes went wide. "But the doctor said ..."

She interrupted him before he could finish. "I'm not talking about that."

She could tell he wasn't following and wanted to provide some context. She told him about a discussion she'd had with Marshall a few days before.

"He was working in the tool shed, and I had gone outside to feed the chickens." She paused and shook her head. "I still can't believe we have chickens now. Who would've thought?" She took a tiny sip of her still-too-hot tea, then continued. "Anyway, we started chatting. You know that I still have moments when I'm waiting for the other shoe to drop, right? I need reassurance that everything I experienced, that we experienced, was real. But also, I just keep wondering—what does it all mean? Does it have to mean something? No, of course not. But ..." She paused. "I have so much to be thankful for, but the fact that I almost lost my son, and then myself, well ... it sure feels like it means something more, you know? Because, Ian, here's the kicker: for the first time in my adult life, I feel whole." She took another sip of her tea. "Anyway, I said all of that to Marshall …"

"You told him all of that?"

"Yeah. I know, it's so strange, but I feel safe talking to him. Don't you?"

Ian nodded.

"When I finished spilling my guts, he said something that stuck with me. I think it was just said in jest—you know, a way to bring it down a notch after my oversharing—because after he said it, he just went right back to his work in the shed, not even pausing for a response."

"Stop keeping me in suspense, Ly, what did he say?"

"He said, 'Maybe the house was trying to show you.'"

"Show you what?" said Ian.

"Exactly what I needed to see?" She looked at Ian.

Ian sipped his coffee, then shrugged. "I'm pretty sure there's an explanation for everything," he said. He lifted his paper and returned to reading.

"You're right."

She blew on her tea again and took a drink.

THIRTY-SEVEN

ZACH STILL HAD lingering questions. He wasn't so quick to dismiss everything that happened to them as circumstantial. For him, it went far beyond the way the house was wired. He had the scars to prove it and each time he looked in the mirror, he was reminded of that very thing.

Before he left for school, he scribbled the phone number he had been meaning to call for months on a piece of paper and slipped it in his pocket.

He knew he only had a short window of time during recess to make the call. He had taken his father's cell phone and stuffed it into his backpack, hoping he wouldn't need it or even know it had gone missing for the time he would have it with him at school.

There was an old wooden picnic table just around the corner, out of sight of the playground, next to one of the doors that led back into the brick school building. It was often used by teachers looking for a break from the chaos of the classroom or to sneak a cigarette. A makeshift ashtray that sat underneath the table sat full of half-smoked cigarette butts.

Zach pulled out the phone and began dialing. He was about to hit the last two remaining numbers, when he was interrupted.

"Is this spot taken?"

Zach tucked the phone underneath his leg and looked up to see Marshall.

"Marshall?" This was the first time he had ever seen him outside of Farr Hill. "What are you doing here?"

Marshall was staring intently at Zach, but not in a creepy way. He seemed deep in thought. It was a look he'd seen on his mother's face many times before. "Working on a project," he said, breaking the silence. "Small repairs, mostly. No electrical wiring, this time," he said, a half-smile appearing on his face. "Apparently I have you to thank."

"What do you mean?"

He opened his mouth to speak, then closed it. A moment later, he answered, "You must have mentioned something to a teacher?"

Zach nodded. He did say something to his English teacher about all the good work Marshall had done at the house. He hadn't mentioned anything about the supernatural stuff, though. He knew better than that.

"I guess I did. Word must travel fast here."

"That's what words do in a small town," said Marshall. He shrugged.

"Well, it's good to see you," Zach added. "It's just … weird seeing you at my school."

"Yeah. Kind of weird being here if you ask me." Marshall looked him right in the eyes.

Zach looked away, feeling guilty for what he almost got caught doing. He wondered how he could end this conversation without tipping that guilt. But then he sighed. He'd been around Marshall enough times to know he couldn't put anything over on him. Marshall must have heard the sigh.

"Why aren't you hanging out with your friends?" Marshall nodded toward the playground where kids were hanging out in small groups, talking, or kicking a ball around. "Something bothering you?"

Zach pulled the phone out from under his leg. "I took it from my dad this morning." He didn't fully disclose his intentions for the phone. He felt bad enough for taking it from his dad.

Marshall sat down next to him on the bench and leaned forward, his hands folded and elbows resting on his knees. The two of them had lots of time together at the house, but this was the first time Zach noticed the tattoo on Marshall's hand. Not only noticed it, but *recognized* it. It was the same symbol that was on the bracelet! He looked down at his wrist, only to remember he'd left the bracelet at home. But that wasn't the whole story. He was sure he'd seen the same symbol elsewhere, too. *At the house?* Why hadn't he figured this out before? Zach was sorting through his foggy memories when Marshall interrupted his thoughts.

"You know, Zach, sometimes the answers are right in front of you."

With that, he stood up and walked to the door, waving goodbye to Zach before heading inside.

Once he was certain Marshall was out of sight, he finished dialing.

"Hello?"

He was nervous and almost hung up. He didn't really know what to say. "Is this Martin, Martin Phillips?"

"This is he."

"Hi, my name is Zach. You don't know me, but my family moved into the house where you used to live. Far Hill? You did live there, right?"

"We did," he said. His voice was calm, but firm. "And moving there was the worst thing that had ever happened to my family. Living in that house tore my family apart. Shortly after leaving, my wife left me. It was too much for us to weather."

Zach was stunned at the honesty of his response.

"You want my advice, kid?" Mr. Phillips asked.

Zach nodded, then realized Mr. Phillips couldn't see his nod over the phone. "Um … yes?"

"Get out of there while you still can."

Just then, the school bell rang, startling Zach. "I'm sorry, but I gotta go."

He hung up, tucked the phone in his pocket, and ran to meet up with the rest of the students walking back to class.

As soon as he and Ariel arrived home from school, Zach was on a mission to return his dad's phone. His parents were both outside, prepping the garden for spring. His timing was perfect. He just needed to make sure Ariel didn't see what he was doing.

She grabbed a granola bar from the pantry, handed one to him, and ran up the stairs to her room.

Zach peered out the door from the kitchen to the garage. The garage door was open. He could see his parents still working on the garden. It was now or never. He ran to Ian's office, threw open the door and started rummaging through papers. Between lecture notes, old newspapers, and books he knew he could find a spot to hide it. He placed it under a stack of papers and put an old newspaper on top of that. He heard the door to the kitchen open and the faint voices of his parents. He double checked his hiding spot and quickly left the room.

Immediately after calling Mr. Phillips, Zach erased the call history. He didn't want anything to be traced back to him should his dad see a strange number on his phone.

"Hey, guys." He peeked his head around the corner into the kitchen. His parents were washing the dirt from their hands.

"How was your day?" his mom asked.

"It was fine. I saw Marshall during lunch break."

"Marshall was there?"

"He's doing some repair work or something," said Zach.

"That's so cool. Maybe you'll get to see a familiar face once in a while."

"Yeah, that would be cool," said Zach. He still hadn't fully adjusted to life at the new school. He was getting there, but slowly. Ironically, the accident helped as he found himself with plenty of new potential friends when he returned. He was "the kid who survived a bee attack". There was novelty in that for the other kids and because of that, Zach felt accepted. This was new for him. A welcome change, for the most part, though sometimes he felt overwhelmed by the increased attention. Still, he could see the good that had come out of everything they'd endured, and that usually satisfied his curiosity on the days when his imagination ran wild.

Today was one of those days.

After Zach finished sharing about his day, he went to his room and replayed the phone conversation from earlier in the day over and over in his head.

It wasn't that bad. Was it? They were unhappy and got divorced, but that happens sometimes, right?

Right?

• • •

In the next room over, Ariel was sitting in the chair in front of her vanity table writing in her journal. When she stopped to take a break and shake out her wrist, she remembered the day months ago when the mirror seemed to melt before her very eyes before shattering into pieces. It had all felt so real.

She shook her head in disbelief and looked at the fully intact and functional mirror, which reflected a clear image of herself. There were still so many unanswered questions. As her mind was overcome with racing thoughts, she paused and looked at her finger.

At the tiny scar that remained.

• • •

"Dinner!"

Zach and Ariel came down to the kitchen at the same time, both wearing sweatpants and curious looks.

"Isn't it a bit early?" Ariel asked.

"Not if we have to drive into town first," Lyana answered. "We're going out tonight. It's been too long since we all had a night out."

"Get dressed kids, we leave in ten minutes." Ian pointed to his watch. "That's ten actual minutes, not ten Ariel or Zach minutes," he added with a half-smile.

"You mean like 'dress up'?" Zach asked?

Lyana pointed to their sweatpants. "I'll accept any outfit that includes actual pants. And maybe a clean shirt?"

Zach and Ariel ran back upstairs. He returned a few minutes later wearing his favorite khaki pants and the only button-down shirt that he claimed fit. Lyana noticed he was also wearing the bracelet Ian had given him. He hadn't worn it in a while.

Fifteen minutes later Ariel sauntered into the kitchen wearing a yellow cashmere sweater and black corduroy skirt she had gotten for Christmas. Her hair was brushed and curled, and she had applied her favorite blush-colored lip gloss.

Zach pointed to his watch. "*That* was ten *Ariel* minutes," he said. She punched him lightly in the arm and started toward the door.

"Well, what's everyone waiting for?" she said. "We better get going."

Lyana couldn't help but smile at the normalcy of it all.

They piled into the car, and the four of them headed to the café. They hadn't been there in months.

When they arrived, they were greeted with a warm smile.

"How's my favorite family?" Lloyd beamed from behind the counter. "Your table is right this way." He motioned toward a four top near the window—the same table they had sat at every weekend after they'd first moved to Littleton.

"Hey, it's our table," said Zach. He scooted over to his favorite seat, one facing the window, then the rest of them slipped into their regular spots around the table.

As the four of them sat around the table, talking and laughing, Lyana looked out the window at Main Street. The streetlights had come on and everything was glowing. The once unfamiliar town full of uncertainty had become home. Faces across the restaurant greeted them with a familiar smile. Passersby on the street waved and nodded. It reminded her of all the reasons why they had moved. It was almost like this place had chosen them, knowing all along exactly what they needed.

She glanced over at Lloyd standing behind the counter, watching them from afar. He was smiling when she caught his eye. He nodded, then offered a thumbs-up.

After a perfect dinner—the kind Lyana had always dreamed of and rarely, if ever, experienced in her own childhood—Lloyd came over to their table.

"Just wanted to thank you for coming tonight," he said. "We've missed you around here."

Lyana stood and offered him a hug.

"It's we who need to thank you for everything you have done for our family." Her voice cracked as a flood of thankfulness threatened to bubble over into tears.

Ian stood and shook Lloyd's hand.

"We really can't thank you enough, Lloyd," he said. He started to get his wallet out, but Lloyd held out his hand.

"No, no. This one is on me."

"But we want to pay ..." began Ian.

"And you will," Lloyd said. "The next time you come in." He lowered his gaze and raised his eyebrows. "Because you will be back, right? Sooner this time?"

Ian laughed and reluctantly put away his wallet.

"Oh, we will, Lloyd."

"You can count on it," added Lyana.

On their way out, Zach stopped to give Lloyd a hug, too. Lyana had to fight tears for the second time that evening. But they were the good kind of tears, so she didn't mind.

• • •

Lloyd watched from the window as they got back into their car.

"The Keane family from Boston," he whispered softly with a smile. The car pulled away and he turned and began cleaning up for the night.

THIRTY-EIGHT

"ZACH, MAKE SURE to shut off the light on your way up," Lyana called out.

She and Ian were in their bedroom with the door open. They had their night stand table lamps on and were already settling into their books. Ian was buried in one of his history books, Lyana had just started a new novel. They would often stay up reading as the kids went to bed. Ariel had turned in early in anticipation of a big test the next day, so they were just waiting on Zach.

Lyana set her book down for a minute and rested her hand on Ian's leg. He placed his book in his lap and grabbed her hand. Ian had often said that they were lucky. He had vowed never to take their relationship for granted. She had promised the same. Through the darkness, they had each managed to find new light. A renewed sense of belonging and purpose.

They returned to their books and went back to reading. Lyana kept an ear to the hallway, listening for his voice. Sure enough, there it was.

"13, 14, 15 …"

There was a long pause, then, "16 … 17 … ?"

Epilogue

*A*S THEY COME *upon the temple, the young boy's father puts him down and instructs him to hide if he sees any strangers approaching. He slips just inside the entrance, next to an offering table made of stone. It is large enough to hide him. He watches as his father speaks with his mother and the High Priestess. The four women quickly gather their baskets and hurriedly follow his father. In the commotion, he sees the High Priestess drop one of her gemstones at the altar. He runs to collect it.*

When he looks up, they are gone. He puts the stone in his pocket and runs to find them. He can see them just ahead in the distance; his father is instructing them to run. His mother turns to see him trailing behind and yells for him to hurry.

They are headed toward the southern gate. Just beyond the gate is an escape tunnel that can get them to the other side of the outer wall. They have prepared for this moment. On the other side of the wall is a small building with enough food and supplies for them to survive for months while they journey south along the river.

The King and the rest of the royal family are waiting for them at a common meeting spot halfway between the temple and the gate. As they reunite, it slows the group just enough so the young boy can catch up. He grabs his mother's hand. Wasting no time, they continue toward their escape route. His father leads the group, protecting the King as is his duty.

The roar from the crowds and the rush of chaos taking over the city echo as they near the gate, which is finally in sight. The fighting has been going on for months and news traveled quickly about troops closing in on the capital. They knew it was only a matter of time before the soldiers overtook the city.

Adrenaline pumps through the young boy. His mother's grip tightens. He can barely see above the adults running in front of him and keeps turning to his mother for reassurance. He looks up as they pass through the gate, focusing on the archway above signifying they are nearly to the tunnel. Just as his eyes return to the scene in front of him, the group comes to a sudden halt. His mother pulls him close.

Waiting for them just outside the gate is a group of bloodthirsty soldiers. The young boy looks around. They are surrounded. Just a few feet separate them from the tips of the soldier's spears, and they have no choice but to stand down. His father extends his arms and tells the group to stay behind him, continuing to protect the King. His mother does the same, protecting her children from the weapons pointed directly at them.

The boy is shuffled to the middle of the group. He peeks around his sisters to catch a glimpse of what is happening. He sees one of the soldiers put his spear down and speak directly to his father.

They have only been standing there a few minutes when he appears. The troops separate to create a path for the man. He is tall and slender. A handsome man. He is the leader of the conquerors, but there is still a gentleness about him. He instructs the soldiers to separate them. The King and his family are taken as a group, along with his father, in one direction. His mother and his sisters are taken in another. As each is grabbed by a soldier, the circle opens. He stands there watching as everyone he loves and the people he has known his entire life are led away, until he is the only one left.

"Akolo!" his mother cries out to him. Her voice is shrill and shaking with fear.

Where are they taking them? Where is my family going? He looks around, confused, frantic.

The tall, handsome man instructs one of the soldiers to take Akolo. He is guided away in a different direction altogether from the others. He can still hear his mother crying for him. He catches his father's eyes, who reassures him with a head nod. And with that nod and the soldier's firm grip around his arm, his mother's screams faded into the distance. He is alone.

He is taken back to the temple. The soldier positions himself in front of the entrance. Akolo curls up and begins sobbing as he waits for what comes next. It isn't the fear of what might happen to him or being held captive by soldiers that scares him. It is the thought of never seeing his family again.

He hears footsteps nearing, then voices. He wipes his eyes and quiets his sobs, anxious to hear what they are saying. The whispers stop when they approach him. The boy sits frozen and silent as he is instructed by the soldiers, not wanting to draw any attention to himself.

The tall, handsome leader of the conquerors is clear with his command. "Keep the boy. We are going to need him."

He turns and walks away.

Akolo is alone.

THE BEGINNING . . .

Acknowledgements and Thanks

Accomplishing the huge feat of completing of our first book could not have been realized without some incredible friends and colleagues who have each played pivotal roles in our own story.

Kalyna Kutny for prodding us forward past our fears and uncertainty. Jennifer Smith for sharing your gifting, direction, experience and creativity. Stephen Parolini for jumping in on the journey and encouraging and inspiring the final spice and flavor. Dan Raines for your wisdom and pushing us even further than we could have imagined. Emily Coey for what so many said couldn't be done—we have lyrics in our story! Aaron and Jen Sanders for being our cheerleaders when we felt like giving up. You believed in us more than we believed in ourselves. And a very special thank you to Amy Grant for providing counsel in our darkest hour that saved us and unlocked this wild story within.

Our greatest gratitude to our God who takes shattered and irreparable pieces and carefully rearranges them to create something unimaginable to change our lives for the good. Hope was whispered in the middle of our darkness.

SERVANT

Book 2

The Goodpasture Chronicles

Sometimes you have to lose everything to find it again.

GoodpastureChronicles.com

About the Author

R.J. Halbert is a husband and wife team who have collaborated on a fantastical story of mystery, suspense, endurance, and triumph in The Goodpasture Chronicles, an adventurous trilogy.

Jason Halbert, one-half of R.J. Halbert, is an Emmy and Grammy Award winning producer and songwriter. His songs have reached millions of listeners worldwide through multiple #1 and Platinum selling albums. In addition to his 20+ year career as Music Director and Producer for Kelly Clarkson, he has left his creative mark on numerous works in film and television, and as well as numerous recording artists over the years. When not creating music, he loves bee-keeping, Sci-Fi, and is known to be quite a storyteller.

After homeschooling their two children around the world on a tour bus, Rhonda Halbert, the second half of R.J. Halbert, has spent the past 10 years as a successful music and television manager, guiding her clients' relationships with labels, networks, and producers. She is also a published photographer, music supervisor, passionate cook, garden enthusiast, and spiritual practitioner.

Together, Jason and Rhonda have woven their 30+ years of life together into a riveting story, based somewhat on truth and experience, but even more so, brimming with imagination.

Learn more at rjhalbert.com